P9-EKS-449

HALF AND HALF

ALSO BY LENSEY NAMIOKA

YANG THE YOUNGEST AND HIS TERRIBLE EAR
YANG THE THIRD AND HER IMPOSSIBLE FAMILY
YANG THE SECOND AND HER SECRET ADMIRERS
YANG THE ELDEST AND HIS ODD JOBS

TIES THAT BIND, TIES THAT BREAK
AN OCEAN APART, A WORLD AWAY

HALF and HALF

LENSEY NAMIOKA

DELACORTE PRESS

I'd like to acknowledge the help of my editor,
Jennifer Wingertzahn, who made some really great suggestions.

Published by
Delacorte Press
an imprint of
Random House Children's Books
a division of Random House, Inc.
New York

Library of Congress Cataloging-in-Publication Data
Namioka, Lensey.
Half and half / Lensey Namioka.
p. cm.
Summary: At Seattle's annual Folk Fest, twelve-year-old Fiona and her older brother
are torn between trying to please their Chinese grandmother and making their
Scottish grandparents happy.
ISBN 0-385-73038-1 (trade)—ISBN 0-385-90072-4 (GLB)
[1. Identity—Fiction. 2. Racially mixed people—Fiction. 3. Chinese Americans—
Fiction. 4. Scottish Americans—Fiction. 5. Family life—Fiction.] I. Title.
PZ7.N1426 Hal 2003
[Fic]—dc21
2002013049

The text of this book is set in 14-point Matrix Book.

Book design by Marci Senders

Printed in the United States of America

June 2003

10 9 8 7 6 5 4 3 2 1

BVG

To my half-and-halves

"Your form isn't complete, Fiona," said the recreations director. "I can't let you enroll in the folk dancing class until it's completely filled in."

The recreation center is located at a park not far from my school. For years the center had been used for adult education classes, such as pottery and language lessons. Recently the building was remodeled and expanded, and they started having classes for young people, too.

When I heard there were folk dancing classes, I immediately went over to enroll. I had never filled out one of their forms before, and I didn't know what the director meant by the form not being completely filled in. I looked it over again.

NAME:	FIONA CHENG
AGE:	11
ADDRESS:	2134 HILLSIDE BLVD. E. SEATTLE, WA
CLASS:	FOLK DANCING

It looked good to me.

"You didn't check a box for race," she said. "To get government funding, we have to let them know how many kids we have in each of the race categories."

This was a problem I'd bumped into before, but I still wasn't sure how to handle it. I took the form from her. "I'll finish it later," I muttered, and quickly left the recreation center.

On the way home, I tried to decide on the best way to complete the form. I had to check one of the boxes that said, "White," "Asian," "Black," "Hispanic," "Native American," or "Other." None of them would be right, though, because I'm not any one of those things. I'm half and half: my father is Chinese and my mother is Scottish. I couldn't just check either "White" or "Asian" since I'm half of each.

I suppose I could have checked the box for "Other," but I didn't want to. It would make me feel like an outsider, a weirdo who didn't belong anywhere. I wanted to fit in like everyone else. Why didn't they have a box for people like me, who were half and half?

When I got home, Mom was in the kitchen, pouring herself a cup of tea. She teaches math at the university, so she's often home in the afternoon. She drinks tea instead of coffee, even though we live in Seattle, the nation's coffee capital. Tea is cheaper than coffee since you can use the tea bag over again. You see, Mom is very thrifty.

She says it's because a mathematician's aim when proving a theorem is to use as little as possible to prove as much as possible. In other words, you always spend a teeny bit to get a whole lot. After doing this for years and years, you wind up being ver-r-r-y thr-r-r-ifty.

I took a seat at the kitchen table. "Mom, what am I?" I asked.

She frowned. "What do you mean? You're Fiona Cheng, last time I looked."

"I'm not asking you *who* I am," I said. "I'm asking you *what* I am."

"What brought this on?" asked Mom, sipping her tea and looking at me over the rim of the cup. I think she suspected that the problem had something to do with our family being racially mixed. It's not something the two of us often discuss.

I told her about the form I had to fill out for the folk dancing class. Mom didn't answer right away. The expression in her hazel eyes didn't tell me much. "Why not check two boxes, one for 'Asian' and one for 'White'?" she suggested after a while.

"I don't think they'll accept that," I sighed. Suddenly I became angry. "Why do grown-ups always have to sort people into boxes anyway?"

"They like to do that, don't they?" said Mom. "But you can't always sort people by the way they look."

To be honest, though, I sorted people, too. Whenever I met another racially mixed kid for the first time, I thought about percentages. I said to myself, "Let's see . . . 65%/35%," meaning that he looks 65% one race and 35% another. Later, when I got to know the person well, I'd forget about the percentage business for the most part. But it was a tough habit to break completely. Maybe I get it from Mom's love of mathematics?

Since Mom wasn't any help, I went upstairs to Dad's studio. He writes and illustrates children's books. His best-known books are a series about a dragon living in ancient China. Dragons are supposed to do all sorts of good things, like bringing rain to lands suffering from drought. But Dad's dragon is secretly scared of water, and just about everything else, too. So how can his dragon present a majestic and fearsome image to the world while preserving his shameful secret? Each of Dad's books puts his dragon in a tight spot, but the dragon always manages to get out of it somehow.

I knew Dad was working on the illustrations for his latest dragon book. Normally I don't like to interrupt him, but this time I needed help.

Dad looked up from his drawing board and placed a large sheet of paper over the picture he was working on. He always does this automatically whenever anyone comes in while he's in the middle of something. He hates having people look at his work before he's satisfied with it.

"What's up, Fiona?" he asked.

I asked him the same question I had asked Mom. "I have to fill out a form for the folk dancing class, and they want to know what race I am. Should I check the box for 'Asian,' or the box for 'White'?"

Dad looked at me. His eyes are a dark brown, just like mine. "Would it bother you to check the box for 'Asian'?" he asked.

"Of course it wouldn't," I said quickly. I've always known that I look more Asian. I have my dad's brown eyes, straight dark hair, and dark skin. By checking the box for "Asian," I would be telling him that I belonged with his people.

"It's just that I have to be accurate," I told Dad. "The recreation center has to report the number of kids they have in each race to get money from the government."

"Then you should do whatever feels right to you," said Dad.

The problem was that I didn't know what felt right to me.

There was only one person left to ask: my brother, Ron. He's twelve years old and has reddish hair and much paler skin than mine. He takes after Mom. I look about 30% white and 70% Asian, while Ron looks maybe 75% white and 25% Asian.

Ron is small for his age, and he's sensitive about his size. He's very conscious that he's exactly the same height as me, even though he's a year older. Mom keeps telling him, "Boys get their growth spurt later, Ron. By the time you're sixteen, you'll overtake Fiona in height."

That's not much comfort to Ron. If you're twelve, sixteen seems an awfully long way off.

Ron used to get picked on by some bullies in school, so Dad had him enroll in kung fu classes to give him confidence. Nobody picks on Ron now. But I know he's still conscious of being one of the shortest boys in his class, and more than anything else, he hates being called a sissy.

I went up to his room. "Say, Ron, you're signing up for the kickboxing team at the recreation center, right?"

He looked up from his homework. "Yeah. So?"

"Have you filled out the form yet?" I asked.

"It's filled out and ready to hand in."

"Which box did you check for race?"

Ron looked at me. His eyes are a light brown, not quite Mom's hazel, but not dark brown like Dad's, either. "Let's see . . . ," he said. "I guess I checked the box for 'Other.'"

"And was that okay with you?" I asked.

"Why should it?" he asked. "None of the other boxes seemed to fit."

"But doesn't that bother you? That anyone who doesn't fit into one of the categories on the form is just lumped into 'Other'?"

Ron shrugged. "I kind of like it when they can't fit me in a box so easily."

It really didn't bother him. Ron didn't mind not belonging. He was perfectly happy to be a loner.

If only it was that easy for me.

Next morning, on the way to the school bus, I still hadn't decided how to fill out my form. If I didn't do it soon, I'd miss the deadline for enrolling in the dance class.

Suddenly I had a brilliant idea: since Ron and I were both half and half, I could check the box for Asian and he could check the box for White.

I was so pleased with my idea that I didn't hear my name being called until I had nearly gotten to the bus stop.

"Hey, wait up, Fiona!"

I turned around and saw my friend Amanda Tanaka. Amanda is Japanese American, and she never has to worry about her race. People think they know all about her since she looks 100% Asian.

I remember the first time I met Amanda. It was a year ago, when our family had moved to Seattle from San Francisco. I was starting school that fall.

Being new, I felt kind of lost. It didn't help that the teacher was also kind of lost. She was a substitute, and she was very young and nervous. Reading the roll, she came to my name and had trouble pronouncing it. "Fee . . . Fee . . . ," She began. Then she looked up at me. "Or is it *Fi,* as in hi-fi?"

There were some snickers from the class. I heard one boy whisper, "Fee fi fo fum, I smell the blood of an Englishman!"

"It's *Fee,*" I said. I took a deep breath and said calmly, "My name is pronounced *Fee-OH-nah.*"

"Really?" said the teacher. "Is it a Chinese name?"

"No," I muttered. "It's Scottish."

"You're Scottish?" asked the teacher, unable to hide her surprise. Somebody giggled.

"I'm half Chinese and half Scottish," I explained for what seemed like the millionth time.

That first day in school seemed to last forever, and I was glad when it was finally over and I was able to escape.

"Is Fiona a common name in Scotland?" asked a voice behind me as I walked toward the school bus.

I turned around and saw a girl from my class who looked Asian.

"It sure is," I told her. "My mom gave me that name because her folks came from Scotland."

"My folks are from Japan, but they didn't try to stick Japanese names on us," said the girl. "I wound up Amanda, and my sister's Melissa."

"Are Japanese names that hard to pronounce?" I asked.

"Some of them are," said Amanda. "I know a girl called Yukiko. Her parents want to make sure everybody knows she's Japanese. Her last name is Kakimoto, so her full name is Yukiko Kakimoto."

I tried to pronounce the name and got tripped up by all the *k*s.

Amanda grinned. "Yukiko has a lot of trouble with people messing up her name. But she's good about it, just like you."

I liked Amanda right away. She made that first day in school seem not so bad after all. We got on the bus together, and we also got off at the same stop.

I saw Amanda again the next day in the lunchroom. I

was joining the line to pick up the hot dish, and after putting it on my tray, I looked around the crowded lunchroom. Where did I fit in? I passed by a table where some kids from my class were seated. One of the boys looked up. "Fee fi fo fum," he whispered to the boy next to him, and they both snickered.

I flashed him my brightest smile. "Hello, Fee-Fi Boy!" I said, and quickly looked for another table. I thought I heard someone laugh.

"Over here!" said Amanda, and I saw her waving at me.

I joined Amanda's table, and this time my smile was real.

Since grown-ups like to put people into boxes, they'd have to call this table the Odds and Ends Box. The kids there included African Americans, Hispanics, whites, Asian Americans, and all sorts of mixtures. It just seemed natural for me to sit at a table where there was variety. Because we were such a mixed bunch, nobody felt different. We were all different and our percentages were all different, too.

Soon after Amanda and I became friends, I pointed out Ron to her. We were in the schoolyard during recess, and

Ron was up on the bars swinging himself along. "That's my brother over there."

Amanda stared at Ron. "Your brother doesn't look like you at all!"

I sighed. "That's what everybody says. He's got that red hair and everything."

From the way Amanda looked at Ron, I suspected she was getting a crush on him. Was it because he looked 75% white? Or maybe she just liked the easy way he swung himself along?

I didn't have the heart to tell her that Ron was basically a loner and would be hard to get to know. In all the time that Amanda and I have been best friends, she and Ron probably haven't exchanged more than twenty words. As far as I remember, "Pass the soy sauce, please" was the only thing he'd ever said to her directly.

While we waited for the school bus, I told Amanda about filling out the form for my dance class. "Would you believe it, I can't enroll in the dance class until I decide what my race is!"

"You're kidding!" she said. "What are you going to do?"

"Ron and I are both signing up for classes," I said. "So I've decided that I'm Asian and he's white. That way, the two of us will average out, and the recreation center will get the right amount of money."

Amanda giggled, and we were still laughing when we got on the bus. After I sat down, I glanced across the aisle. That was when I got a shock.

The boy sitting across the aisle was Harry Kim, a Korean American boy who sat at our lunch table. That day he looked so different that I didn't recognize him at first. He had bleached his black hair a light blond.

It got me thinking. What would happen if I dyed my hair, too? All my dolls were blondes or redheads, with long, long legs. In most movies and TV shows, the women have blond hair and very blue eyes. Obviously this is how most girls want to look.

With Harry's Asian features, the combination was kind of exotic. But I still couldn't decide whether or not I liked it. Since my own features were 70% Asian, I'd look exotic if I dyed my hair, too.

Amanda was also looking at Harry. "My sister Melissa has been talking about dyeing her hair blond. She and my mom had a terrible fight about it."

"Why won't your mom let her?" I asked. "I see lots of kids with dyed hair, not just Harry."

"Mom says Melissa wants to change her hair to blond because she wants to deny her Asian heritage and try to look white."

I don't always get along with Melissa. She's usually in a sour mood, and when I go over to Amanda's house, Melissa calls me "That Scotch Girl" in a sneering kind of way.

But this time I was on Melissa's side. "Your mom's not being fair. Lots of white kids bleach or dye their hair, sometimes in really weird colors, too. Black hair is so boring! Maybe Melissa just wants to show her independence, or make a fashion statement."

Amanda looked thoughtful. "I wonder if my mom would still say no if Melissa wanted to dye her hair blue or green. Then she couldn't accuse her of trying to look white."

"What if I dyed *my* hair red?" I asked.

Amanda laughed. "Well, you'd be denying only half of your heritage since half of you is Scotch."

If I did dye my hair red, would my percentage go from 30%/70% to 50%/50%? That way my outside would match my inside percentages better.

Then I remembered one good reason not to change my hair. Nainai was coming to visit soon, and she would be staying with us for a few days.

Nainai is what Ron and I call our Chinese grandmother. It's the Chinese word for your father's mother. There is a different Chinese word for your *mother's* mother, and that's *waipo*. But I don't call my other grandmother *waipo*, because she wouldn't understand. My mother's parents are the MacMurrays, and they came over from Scotland thirty years ago, when Mom was only five years old.

Mom still speaks with a bit of a Scottish accent. My

friends think it's cute, but frankly I wish she wouldn't roll her *r*s quite so hard. I think she does it on purpose.

Nainai has an accent, too, but since she spent most of her life in China, I don't mind it so much. She tells great ghost stories, and her Chinese accent makes them sound even scarier.

"Nainai will have to sleep in your room when she visits," Mom told me. "She'll have your bed, and you can use your sleeping bag. I know you won't mind."

Mom was right. I didn't mind sharing my room with Nainai. She and I are close. I love the way she smiles at me and says, "You look more and more like your father."

Dad is Nainai's favorite son, so this is a real compliment. That's why Nainai would have a terrible shock if I dyed my hair red. She might be hurt, because she would think that I was trying to look like my mom instead of my dad.

Nainai had to share my room because Mom's parents, the MacMurrays, were coming, too, and they'd be using the guest room. They were coming down from Vancouver, British Columbia, for the annual Folk Fest.

The Folk Fest is held once a year during a weekend in

spring, and it's when all the ethnic groups in our region put on programs showing their arts, crafts, costumes, food, drama, dance, and music. Our teachers and the local papers and TV are always talking about how "ethnically diverse" Seattle is, and the Folk Fest is supposed to show off our diversity. Our family goes every year and we squeeze in as many shows as we can. In three days you can see performances from every continent on earth, from countries I hadn't even heard of.

This year Grandpa MacMurray had been invited to direct some of the Scottish dancing at the Folk Fest. Music and dancing are his two great loves—maybe that's where I got my own love of dancing. Over the years, Grandpa has taken part in many dance programs in Vancouver, but this was the first time he'd be doing one in Seattle.

Since Grandpa and Grandma live close by—Vancouver is only about 150 miles away—they visit us so often that we've gotten into the habit of thinking of the guest room as *their* room.

This wouldn't be the first time my father's and my mother's parents met. They were all there for my parents' wedding, of course, and they met during the holidays a few times. But they never had to stay together in the same house for long. Dad's parents usually stayed at a hotel when they came up from San Francisco to visit.

But since Dad's father died last year, we always invite Nainai to stay with us when she is in town, since we don't want her to be in a hotel all by herself. Lots of other single women do it, of course. But Nainai looks kind of soft and helpless, and we can't stand the thought of her drifting around, lonely and lost, in a big downtown hotel.

So that was why Nainai would be sharing my room three days from now. It would also be the first time she and Mom's parents would be spending more than a week together.

I didn't think there'd be a problem. Grandpa and Grandma MacMurray are happy people who like to laugh a lot and make jokes.

If I was worried about anything during my grandparents' visit, it was with Dad. Normally, I enjoy being Fiona Cheng, daughter of Frank Cheng, the writer and illustrator of children's books. It always gives me a thrill when one of my friends says to me, "I just loved your father's latest! When is he going to do another Cowardly Dragon book?"

My brother Ron and I try to think up ideas for Dad, but in the end he always comes up with the best ones himself. So I'm proud of my dad—most of the time. It's just when Nainai comes to visit that I feel embarrassed. For some reason, he starts acting like a child when she's around.

I began to notice this during Nainai's visit last year. It was her first after our grandfather had died, so it was the first time she came alone. When both my Chinese grandparents were here, the men usually hung out together. Dad, Grandfather, and Ron would sit in the living room while Nainai, Mom, and I prepared food in the kitchen. Actually, it was Nainai who did the cooking, while Mom and I looked on.

But during this visit, things were different. Dad didn't have his father to talk with, so he came into the kitchen and joined Nainai. Since he normally did the cooking anyway, this seemed perfectly natural. It was the way he talked to her when they were in the kitchen that was so strange.

I noticed first of all that his voice sounded higher than usual. Even worse, I heard him calling her Ma. He sounded like a doll I used to have that said "Ma" when you pressed its stomach.

Later that evening, he brought Nainai all his newest drawings and sketches. That surprised me, because he never showed his sketches to *us*. I don't think even Mom saw them. Dad stood there patiently waiting while Nainai slowly looked over his work.

Nainai frowned at one of the drawings. She pointed to a corner and said, "*Bu dui.*"

Although I know very little Chinese, I did understand this phrase, which means "Not right."

Dad just bowed his head meekly and accepted her comment. It reminded me of the times when Ron and I brought home our report cards and stood nervously waiting while our parents looked them over and made comments. It's okay for Ron and me, but it was different when I saw my dad, a grown man, doing it.

Mom noticed me looking on. I must have made a face, because she called me over and took me to her bedroom. "Why does it bother you, Fiona, when your father is so anxious to please Nainai?" she asked. "What's wrong with a child wanting his parent to be proud of him?"

"But that's just the point!" I said. "He's a grown-up! He looks so silly, behaving like a child again!"

Mom sighed and patted the space next to her on the bed. When I sat down, she looked at me for a moment with her hazel eyes, then turned away and played with a curl of her hair. She always does that when she's not quite sure what to say. I love the way her red hair curls naturally.

Finally Mom broke her silence. "Ever since your father and I met, we kept discovering unexpected things about each other. Most of these had to do with differences between Chinese and Western customs."

"Why did you decide to marry a Chinese anyway?" I asked. "You must have had a lot of white boyfriends."

Then I was worried that Mom would be offended by my question. Maybe it was one that Grandpa and Grandma MacMurray had asked, too. Had they been shocked and unhappy when Mom told them she was planning to marry a Chinese man?

Mom didn't look offended. "By the time we decided to get married, I no longer thought of your father as Chinese, particularly. After you get to know people, you don't think about their race anymore. You'll find this out for yourself someday."

I'd already found this out. Most of the time I don't think of Amanda as Japanese American. She's just my friend. But making friends with a person isn't the same thing as actually marrying him.

"How did you and Dad meet?" I asked Mom. "How long did it take you to get to know each other and fall in love?" I had heard this story many times, but I loved hearing it over and over again.

"Your father and I first met in college, when a bunch of us went to a city hall meeting. We were protesting because the city wanted to close a park near the campus."

"So then what happened?"

"The speeches got boring after a while, and I started looking around," Mom continued. "I saw that the student next to me was busily scribbling in his notebook. I thought at first that he was taking notes. Then I saw that he was drawing funny sketches of the speakers. He was making them all into animals—cats, dogs, pigs, goats . . . I burst out laughing. He laughed, too, and we made so much noise that an usher escorted us out. That was how your dad and I got acquainted."

"So you decided to start dating?"

"Not right away, even though we liked each other. It was two years before we finally decided to get married. By then I thought I really knew your father pretty well, and that there'd be no surprises left."

I saw her lips give a little twist. When she does that, I never know whether she's amused or mad. "So what were some of the surprises?" I asked.

This time I saw a real smile. "One of them was seeing your father behaving like a child with his parents," she said. "At the wedding reception, he kept running up to them and asking if the food was all right. And all the time he was the groom!"

"That must have made you mad," I said. Poor Mom! I was surprised she could laugh about it now.

And she *was* laughing, too. "Fortunately I had other things to think about," she continued. "Later, much later, I did ask your father why he went into the little boy act whenever he saw his parents, especially his mother. He was astounded, because he never realized that he did it. Finally he said that it was probably just filial duty." She looked at me. "Do you know what that is?"

I shook my head.

"Filial duty means children paying a debt to their parents for bringing them up."

"So filial duty is important to the Chinese?" I asked.

Mom nodded. "It's considered one of the most important virtues, if not *the* most important. Your dad told me a famous Chinese story about a man whose parents were growing old and feeble. To make them feel better, he began to drool and crawl on the ground and babble like a baby. He wanted them to feel that they were young parents of a newborn baby."

I couldn't believe my ears. "Gosh! Is that really a true story?"

"Whether it's true or not, this man is always held up in China as an example of an outstanding son," said Mom.

If this was how the Chinese thought a good son should behave, maybe they *were* a lot different from me.

I didn't look forward to seeing Dad being a good son

when Nainai came for this visit. It would be especially embarrassing this time, because Grandpa and Grandma MacMurray were visiting, and they might see the way Dad behaved toward Nainai. They loved a good laugh, and I usually loved laughing with them.

But not if they were laughing at Dad.

On Tuesday, three days before the start of the Folk Fest, Grandpa and Grandma MacMurray arrived.

Ron and I heard a car pull up outside soon after we got home from school. We heard Grandpa's booming laugh, and by the time we got to the front door, Grandpa and Grandma were coming up the steps with their suitcases. They were not people who stood around wasting time.

Grandpa gave Ron a crushing hug and pounded him on the back. "Well, look here!" he cried. "If it isn't Fu Manchu himself!"

Fu Manchu was a Chinese villain in some old books popular in the 1930s, and even now he is still held up as an example of the sinister Oriental. But Ron only laughed. It was an old joke between him and Grandpa. Since Ron has reddish hair and Mom's freckles, he doesn't look anything like Fu Manchu, with his long mustache, sallow skin, and slanted eyes.

Grandma ran up to give me a hug. "Hello, Fiona, lass. My, you've grown another three inches since we last saw you."

Since she had seen me only a month ago, I knew this wasn't true. Grandma loves to exaggerate, and if she had said I'd grown only two inches, I would have been insulted.

Ron and I helped carry our grandparents' luggage up to the guest room. Naturally we stuck around while they unpacked. I'd be a liar if I said I wasn't expecting them to bring gifts. From Grandpa's suitcase came a pleated woolen skirt in the MacMurray tartan, which I had learned to recognize.

"Wow!" I cried, snatching the skirt and holding it up to my waist. It was just the right length for me.

"It's not for you, Fiona!" said Grandpa. "Don't you know that kilts are for laddies?"

He held the kilt out to Ron, who turned pink as he accepted the gift and mumbled his thanks.

Next, Grandpa took out a leather purse and a cap. Again, I started to reach out, but they turned out to be for Ron, too. "This purse is called a sporran," Grandpa told him, "and you hang it from your waist so it dangles in front. The cap is called a Balmoral."

Ron's embarrassment almost made up for my disappointment.

"Hey, Ron," I cried, "let's see you put the whole outfit on so you can show off to your friends!"

"I told you the poor lad would be embarrassed, Alec," Grandma said to Grandpa. "This is America! What would he do with a kilt here?"

"He can wear it and be proud of it!" declared Grandpa. "We MacMurrays have worn the kilt for hundreds of years!"

"Nonsense," Grandma said. "The kilt wasn't even invented until the eighteenth century."

Ron brightened up. "Really? So Scottish men didn't always wear it?"

"That doesn't make it any less authentic!" insisted

Grandpa. After a moment, he grinned sheepishly and added, "But your grandma's right. Some factory owner or another discovered that the long plaid his workers wore kept getting caught in the machinery. So he made them wear a shorter garment. And that's how the kilt was developed."

Grandma turned to me. "And this is your gift, Fiona. Your mother told me what you needed, and I got the biggest one I could find."

She held out a big pink clay pig. I was born in the Year of the Pig, according to the Chinese calendar, and I've got lots of stuffed pigs, tiny pig figurines, and of course greeting cards with nothing but pigs. I was delighted to add Grandma's clay pig to my collection. It wore a huge, smug grin, and I found myself grinning back at it. "Thank you, Grandma!" I said.

"It's a bank," said Grandma. "Your mother said it's time for you to learn how to save money."

Then I noticed that there was a slit on the back of the pig. Suddenly the expression on the pig's face looked a lot less friendly. It became demanding. "Put your allowance in here!" it said. "Stop wasting money!" it said.

Mom likes to say that she comes from a long line of thr-r-r-ifty people, since the Scots have a reputation for being great savers. But Grandpa and Grandma MacMurray aren't nearly as stingy as Mom. She gets it also from being a mathematician. It's probably just Mom's way of having fun.

It can be really embarrassing when we go out to a restaurant with other families and the waitress comes with the bill. Mom is always asked to figure out how much each family owes because she's the mathematician. She takes *ages* to figure everything down to the last penny while the waitress stands there looking patient. At times like that, I want to crawl under the table and die.

Once, another mother lost her patience and said, "Why don't I just pay for everything? You can do it next time."

But Mom wouldn't hear of it. "I don't want to pay a penny *less* than what I owe. But I don't want to pay a penny *more,* either."

It's almost as embarrassing when it's Mom's turn to drive Amanda and me to the library on weekends. We'd drive around and around and around looking for a parking place.

"Hey, there's a space!" Amanda yells. But Mom won't take it. She has to find a parking place with time left on the meter.

"Instead of saving," I tried to point out to her once, "I bet you spend a lot more money on gas from the extra driving."

But Mom just laughed. "It's the principle of the thing."

When she goes shopping, Mom brings her old brown paper shopping bags, which she's used and reused until the brown paper becomes soft and almost furry. Once, Amanda went to the store with us, and as she helped us carry the groceries, she looked at her bag with wonder. "Wow, this bag must be really ancient!"

"All of Mom's bags are at least three years old," I said, gingerly supporting my bag of groceries against my chest.

"You're reusing old paper bags because you want to save a tree, don't you, Mrs. Cheng?" said Amanda. "That's great! Our teacher says that using a lot of plastic bags is bad for the environment, too."

"Mom's really doing it because the store gives her

back a nickel when she brings her own paper bags," I told Amanda.

"Thr-r-r-rift!" said Mom, and winked. She looked very young when she said this, making me feel almost like her older sister. Saving money is a game Mom loves to play, and being both a thrifty Scot and a mathematician is just an excuse.

But sometimes I just wish she'd act like other people's mothers.

Maybe Mom liked to play saving games, but I didn't. Still, I took the piggybank from Grandma and tried to look grateful.

Grandma seemed to read my mind. "Put in mostly coins," she suggested with a wink. "They make a bigger clatter than paper money."

Dad came home a little while later and greeted Grandpa and Grandma MacMurray warmly. He's always gotten on well with them, even if he finds them puzzling sometimes.

They get along well with him, too, but they find him just as puzzling. I've seen their jaws literally drop.

Once, Grandpa MacMurray showed off a new cashmere scarf he had bought.

Dad admired it, then asked, "How much did it cost?"

"It cost quite enough," Grandpa said stiffly.

Afterward, I overheard Mom saying to Grandpa, "Frank didn't mean to be nosy. The Chinese often ask people how much things cost. It's their way of showing appreciation."

Grandpa shook his head in bewilderment. "I'll have to get used to it, I suppose."

I hate to think how bewildered Grandpa and Grandma MacMurray would be if Dad ever used baby talk with them. Fortunately, he hasn't tried it yet.

Another thing they can't figure out is why Dad does most of the cooking—not only that, but he seems to enjoy it. Tonight Dad went straight into the kitchen after greeting them. Soon I could hear the sounds of the fridge door opening, the faucet being turned on, and the clatter of pots and pans being taken out.

Grandma looked at me. "Aren't you going to help your pa, Fiona?" she asked.

"Dad doesn't like people getting in his way," I explained. "Later, I'll help set the table, and Ron and I will do the dishes, of course."

For as long as I can remember, Dad has always done the cooking. It wasn't until Grandpa and Grandma MacMurray mentioned it that I realized this was unusual, and that in most families the mother did the cooking.

Dad prefers to do the cooking because he gets home earlier from his job, which is working as a translator for a company that does business with China. He has only a part-time job so that he has time to work on his books.

Since Mom teaches full-time and usually comes home later than Dad, she's glad to have him do the cooking. Ron and I are happy about it, too. Mom is a lousy cook. When Dad has to go away to give talks at schools and libraries, Ron and I usually beg Mom to take us to some fast-food place.

Mom came home just as I was setting the table. As she greeted her parents her Scottish accent became a lot stronger. In fact I had trouble understanding some of their talk.

It didn't take long to exchange news, since we see Grandpa and Grandma once every other month, either when they come down here or when we drive up to Vancouver.

"Do you want to do some shopping or go to the art museum?" Mom asked as we sat down to dinner. "The Folk Fest doesn't start for another three days."

"We'll be needing all three days for the dancers to practice," said Grandpa. "Would it be all right with you if we rehearse right here in this house? Eight youngsters jumping up and down can produce a great deal of noise."

Mom smiled. "I'm used to the noise. I grew up with it, remember? There's enough space here in the living room, if we roll the rug back."

I was really excited, because this would give me a chance to see the dancers practicing, instead of just watching the actual performance. "I'd love to join the dancing someday," I said.

Then I noticed that Grandma was looking at me with a huge smile. "You're about to get your wish, darling," she said. "One of our dancers had to drop out at the last minute, and she felt terrible about it. But I told her I know of a substitute right here in Seattle."

It took me a moment to understand what she meant. *I* was going to be the substitute! I wanted to whoop and start dancing right that minute. My happiness was complete when Grandma said, "For the dance, you'll be wearing Ron's kilt."

"You'll only be wearing it for the dance, mind," Grandpa told me. "Afterward, you'll have to return it to your brother."

I nodded. I was so happy about joining the dancing that I didn't mind the thought of giving up the kilt immediately afterward.

I know a little Scottish dancing. Once, Grandpa and Grandma took Ron and me to a Scottish festival in Vancouver called the Highland Games, and I immediately fell in love with the dancing. When I saw the dancers leaping in the air, I wanted to bounce with joy.

The dance that impressed me the most was the one where the dancer hopped repeatedly over a pair of crossed swords on the ground. Grandpa told me it was called *Gillic Calum.* The dancer skipped so neatly and lightly that it looked easy, but I knew it must be very hard, even dangerous. Yet the dancer looked like he was having a great time. Maybe the danger added to the excitement.

Afterward, I begged Grandpa to teach me the steps of some Scottish dances. He absolutely refused to teach me the sword dance, no matter how hard I tried to persuade him. I wondered whether he refused because it was too dangerous or because I was a girl. What if Ron had asked Grandpa to teach him the sword dance?

Of course Ron hadn't asked. At the Highland Games, Ron hadn't gone to any of the dances, only to the sports games.

But Grandpa hadn't given up on getting Ron into his troupe at this year's Folk Fest. "Don't you want to give the dancing a try, Ron?" he asked. "You'll like it! I've seen how light you are on your feet."

Ron shook his head and said quickly, "I'll be too busy to practice. I promised my teacher to help coach some of the younger boys in my kung fu class."

Grandpa sighed. "All right, I won't force you."

I couldn't help feeling jealous. Ron was Grandpa's redheaded laddie, the one who, by rights, should be wearing the kilt.

It made me feel better when Grandma said, "Fiona will do splendidly in the dance. I just know it."

Ron was more cheerful, too. Not only was he safe from the dancing, he was also saved from the kilt. "Our family is going to be really involved in the Folk Fest this year," he said.

"Who else is going to take part?" asked Grandma.

"I'm going to compete in the junior division of the kung fu exhibition bouts on Saturday morning," said Ron.

I knew he was very proud that his team had been chosen to compete. For weeks, Ron had been talking about the kung fu exhibition at the Folk Fest, and he had been practicing furiously. There was a good chance that he might win his bout in the exhibition.

Dad spoke up. "We'll all be busy at the festival. I've been asked to talk at a session about children's books by local authors."

I felt a surge of pride. Dad is a good speaker, funny in his quiet way, and the kids love him. But why hadn't he told us sooner?

That was exactly what Grandpa MacMurray said. "Why did you keep the news to yourself until now, Frank?"

Dad smiled. "Well, it's supposed to be a surprise, but since everybody else is talking about the festival, I couldn't resist coming out with the news."

Why did he have to keep it a surprise? I began to suspect there was more to Dad's talk than he was telling us.

Anyway, this year's Folk Fest was going to be one of the best ever for our family. I didn't see how anything could spoil it.

As soon as I came home from school on Wednesday, Grandpa began to teach me the dances we'd be doing at the festival. I had taken some folk dancing classes, but I still had to practice before I was ready to join the other dancers coming over that evening.

Footwork wasn't the only thing I needed work on. I also had to know how to hold my hands: when to raise which one over my head, and when to keep them on my waist (Grandpa called this position "akimbo"). The fingers had to be just right, too.

Grandpa's troupe consisted of eight dancers, and our program would start with some Highland reels. I already knew the steps of the reel: advance right foot, close with left foot, advance right and hop, then advance left, and so on. What I needed was practice doing the steps in loops that wound back and forth, which were typical of reels.

I also needed drilling on the way to move my shoulders so that I could pass another dancer back to back without the two of us bumping into each other. Under Grandpa's directions, I spent some time trying to move lightly and easily, and to look as if I was having a good time. Actually, I *was* having a good time, but making it look easy wasn't easy.

After dinner, Grandma helped me put on my costume for the dance. At last, I got to put on Ron's kilt!

"I don't know what the world is coming to," grumbled Grandpa when he saw me all dressed up in the kilt and blouse and wearing the sporran and Balmoral cap.

"You have to face reality, Alec," Grandma told him. "Nowadays you can't find many boys who like to dance."

Strictly speaking, we were supposed to be four boys and four girls for most of the dances. But even in Vancouver, Grandpa's troupe always had fewer boys than girls, so he had to have some girls dressed as boys. Everybody wore plaid skirts and frilly blouses and the same kind of bonnet, and from a distance, you couldn't tell the boys from the girls.

The whole troupe of dancers came over after dinner. Including me, our group consisted of five girls and three boys. Most of the dancers were not much older than I was. Grandpa told me that he was in charge of the younger group, but there was also another troupe of older dancers doing more complicated stuff.

Looking around at the other dancers, I couldn't help noticing that they looked very different from me. They all had brownish or red hair and pale skin. Several had freckles. My black hair and darker skin really stood out in the crowd. I tried not to let it bother me.

We started practicing in the living room, and soon the

whole house shook as we thumped and stamped and hopped and skipped. Besides coaching us on the dancing, Grandpa provided the music with his fiddle. Once, I called his instrument a violin, and he corrected me. "I'm a fiddler, not one of your stuck-up violinists!" he declared. Fiddler or violinist, he was good, and the tunes just leaped off his instrument and set our feet jumping to keep time.

Even after a whole afternoon of practicing with Grandpa, dancing with the others was a challenge. I didn't have too much trouble making my feet do the right steps and keeping my arms in the right position. But I saw what Grandpa meant about being in the right place at the right time. Soon after we began, I bumped into another dancer—a girl about my age with curly ginger hair. She just smiled and kept on dancing. After that, I concentrated harder and managed not to bump anybody again.

I love all kinds of dancing, and I was a little disappointed that Dad couldn't teach me any Chinese dances. "Chinese farmers did some folk dancing, usually connected with rice planting or harvesting," he said. "But most other dances were done by professionals in the old days."

"What about now?" I asked. "Is there much dancing in China these days?"

Dad smiled. "Actually, many Chinese in the cities prefer Western ballroom dancing!"

So that's why I don't know any traditional Chinese dances. I do know some American folk dances, but I still think the Scottish dances are the most fun. As we rehearsed in our living room, I could almost imagine myself leaping around in the purple heather.

After an hour of dancing, Grandpa called for a break. His face was streaming with sweat, his thatch of red-gray hair was standing on end like a rusty Brillo pad, and his eyes were shining. He loves dancing as much as I do, and I was determined to make him proud of me, even though he really wanted Ron, not me, to be in the dance troupe.

At the thought of Ron, I looked around and found him sitting on the sofa with Grandma. Both of them had been watching the rehearsal. One of the boys in the group went over to Ron, and the two of them started talking.

"Hey, why aren't you dancing?" the boy asked.

Ron grinned, looking a bit embarrassed. "The dancing

looks okay, but I don't know if I can manage all that hopping while wearing a skirt."

"It's not a skirt," protested the boy. "It's a kilt."

"Skirt, kilt, what's the difference?" said Ron.

"I know what's bothering you," said the boy. "You're afraid people will think you're a sissy. Well, let me tell you . . ."

I noticed that Grandpa had been listening to the exchange. Now he moved forward. "Come on, let's get back to the practice," he said. "We don't have time to waste, and we have to do better in that last reel. Some of you were falling behind in your hops."

After another hour of practicing, we were really exhausted. Grandpa declared that we had practiced enough for the night, and we all flopped down on the floor and groaned with relief. I struggled up and helped Grandma serve juice and cookies to the dancers.

I started talking to the girl I had bumped into earlier. "Hi, I'm Maggie Guthrie," she said. "This is my first time with the Scottish dance troupe. How about you?" Maggie's ginger-colored curls now hung limp with sweat.

"I'm Fiona Cheng," I told her. "This is my first time, too."

Maggie took a cookie and looked curiously at me. "You're Chinese, aren't you? Do you know any Chinese dances?"

"No, my dad hasn't taught me any Chinese dances," I said lightly. "But I think Scottish dancing is more fun than any other kind. And I'm half Scottish too," I couldn't help adding.

Although I tried not to show it, I was bothered by her question. Normally I don't mind looking Chinese. But now I was very conscious that I didn't belong. I felt like a prune in a bowl of strawberries.

I began to think it would help if I did dye my hair. It would make me fit in a little better with the rest of the troupe. And I was tired of feeling left out. I wanted to blend in for a change.

At school on Thursday, I told Amanda I was thinking of dyeing my hair. She stared at me. "Do you really mean it?"

"I'm dancing in my grandfather's troupe," I told her.

"All the other kids have red or auburn hair. One boy has light brown hair, but nobody has black hair like me."

"But what will your folks say?" asked Amanda.

"I don't want them to know until it's all done," I said. Before I lost my nerve, I quickly added, "I need your help, Amanda. Can I come over after school and dye my hair at your house?"

Amanda gulped. "Okay. Maybe we can get Melissa to help. Like I told you, she's been thinking about dyeing her hair, but she still hasn't made up her mind to do it." After a moment, she said, "Maybe seeing you do it will help her decide."

Before going to the Tanakas' after school, Amanda and I went to the nearest drugstore to buy some hair dye. I found so many different kinds of dyes that I had no idea what to get. "What color are you trying for?" asked Amanda. It was a good question. I just wanted something that wouldn't make me stick out in the dance troupe. "Well, maybe I should aim for Ron's hair color."

Mom's hair is a fiery red, but Ron's hair is closer to the color on the package labeled "chestnut." So that was what I wound up buying.

We found Melissa at home. As usual, she looked at me without much friendliness. But her expression changed when Amanda said, "Fiona wants to dye her hair red, Melissa. Can you help her with the dyeing?"

Melissa broke into a smile. "Sure! Hey, when my mom sees how nice your hair looks, maybe she'll change her mind and let me dye mine."

We got to work. Actually, it was Melissa who did all the work, while Amanda stood around getting in everybody's way in the crowded bathroom. Melissa put on a pair of rubber gloves that came with the kit and squeezed the goo from the tube of dye. Underneath the strong perfume, I could tell there was another smell, something chemical. I didn't know what it was, and I didn't want to know.

After all the goo was used up and worked into my hair, Melissa stood back and looked at me thoughtfully. "Hmm . . . your hair still looks awfully dark. Maybe it's because it was almost black to start with."

"We probably have to wait a little before the color changes," suggested Amanda.

We waited for about ten minutes, while I sat on the edge of the bathtub and peeked at the mirror every so often. It was pretty uncomfortable. The package said to wait for forty-five minutes, but shouldn't the color be redder by now?

"I've got an idea," Melissa said to me. "I have a package of dye for blond hair. That's the color I've been thinking of using. Why don't we put some of that stuff on your hair? It should lighten your color a bit."

"I don't know," said Amanda. "Better not take a chance."

I looked in the mirror again. My hair was still dark brown, not Ron's chestnut. "Okay, let's try it," I said.

So Melissa opened her tube of dye and worked some of it into my hair. "Hey, I'm beginning to see a difference," she said after a few minutes.

I looked in the mirror. She was right. My hair was definitely lighter. Then things began to happen, and happen fast.

"It's red enough now!" yelled Amanda. "Isn't there some way to stop the dyeing?"

"We'd better rinse!" said Melissa.

I leaned over the washbasin while Melissa ran hot water over my head. "Ouch! That's too hot!" I cried.

"The water has to be hot enough to stop the dyeing," panted Melissa.

After some furious rinsing and massaging, Melissa stopped the water. "It's not going to change any more," she said. Her voice was shaking badly, and that really scared me.

What scared me even more was the sight of Amanda. She was hunched over, with her hands covering her face.

I took a deep breath, and slowly raised my eyes to look in the mirror.

You know when you scoop some orange Jell-O into a bowl and it's still wobbling? That was how my hair looked, as I stood there trembling and stared at myself. I swear that my hair would have glowed in the dark if we'd turned the lights off.

So much for blending in.

After a long silence, Melissa cleared her throat. "Maybe we should go back to the store and get some dark-brown dye."

"I don't need to dye again, because I'm already going to die when my family sees this," I said hoarsely. "Anyway, it's late and I have to go home."

My feet began to drag as I approached our front door. What was I going to say to Dad and Mom? To Ron? To Grandpa and Grandma MacMurray? If my hair had turned out chestnut, I could have explained that I wanted to look like part of the dance troupe. But how do you explain orange Jell-O?

Ron was the first person I met in the house. He stared. "You've got to be kidding!" he said. "What were you thinking?"

"I guess I was thinking I needed a change."

"It's a change all right. You look like a tree with leaves that are turning bright orange and falling off. Is your hair going to fall off too?" Then he laughed and went into the kitchen to fix himself a snack. It would never occur to him that I might want to have hair the same color as his.

The next person I met was Grandma. She was sitting in the living room, and when she saw me, she put her hand over her mouth. "Oh, my poor Fiona!"

Laughter I was prepared to face, but sympathy was too

much. My mouth trembled, and I could feel hot tears welling up.

"Come here, darling," said Grandma. She pulled me over to the sofa and sat down next to me, putting her arms around my shoulders. "I suppose it's too late to change? The dye is permanent?"

"I'm stuck with it until my hair grows out!" I wailed. "It will take years!"

"Not years, only months," she said, giving me her handkerchief.

That wasn't much comfort. I honked into the handkerchief, which became a soggy mess. "I dyed my hair because I want to belong to the troupe," I said, sniffling. "I want to look like a Scottish dancer!"

Grandma's arms tightened around me. "Listen, Fiona, not all Scots have red hair. In fact some have dark hair, as dark as yours."

I sat up. "I didn't know that!"

"Before the Celts arrived in Scotland, there were people living there called Picts," said Grandma. "They were a smaller, darker people. They had mostly dark hair and spoke a different language."

I had thought that Scottish people were all big and fair, and looked like Grandpa and Grandma MacMurray. I wiped my eyes with Grandma's soggy handkerchief. "Are there many Picts left?" I asked.

"You still see people in Scotland who are small and dark, especially in the Highlands," said Grandma. "Your dark hair wouldn't have looked too out of place."

"Then why is Grandpa so anxious for Ron to be one of the dancers?" I asked.

"Let me explain," said Grandma. "Your grandpa loved to dance. He was a notable dancer in his youth. The name Alec MacMurray meant something in the world of Scottish dance."

I tried to picture Grandpa leaping around in a kilt.

"Oh, you should have seen him when he was young!" said Grandma, her eyes sparkling. Then she sighed. "Your grandpa had always hoped that someday he would have a boy who would love dancing as much as he did."

"Instead, you had Mom," I said softly.

"We're both very proud of your mother," said Grandma. "Don't think for a minute that we're sorry we never had a son!"

"But Mom doesn't care much about Highland dancing, does she?" I said.

Grandma gave me another hug. "And you do. How you look doesn't matter, Fiona. The only thing that matters is that you're a grand dancer. Grandpa will find that out soon enough."

"Find what out?" said Grandpa, coming into the living room.

"Guess," said Grandma, and she winked at me.

I waited for Grandpa to say something about my hair, but he just looked at me for a second and then said, "Better do your homework now, Fiona. We have more rehearsing to do this evening."

Did he notice my hair? Would he even notice if my hair was the color of a red traffic light that blinked on and off?

I went upstairs and tried to do my homework, but I soon gave up because I couldn't concentrate. Dad was due home any minute and I couldn't stop thinking about what his reaction would be. Would he be hurt and angry because he'd think I was trying to look more Scottish and less Chinese? Of course that wasn't the real reason I'd dyed my hair. I'd never do anything to hurt Dad's feelings. I just wanted to look like everyone else.

Dad came home twenty minutes later. I was waiting near the front hall so he would see me immediately and get it over with.

When he came in the door, he just stared at me silently. I couldn't read his expression, and my heart was thumping as I waited for him to say something.

"I'm glad you didn't change your features, anyway," he said finally.

I didn't understand what he meant by that. Change my features? I may have dyed my hair, but even with permanent dye, nothing was really permanent. My hair would grow back its real color. I hadn't actually changed anything about myself. Couldn't Dad see that? At least he didn't look angry or upset. That was a huge relief.

I spent the next half hour trying to figure out the best way to wear my new hair. Finding a style that suited it wasn't easy. I'd already seen the bowl of Jell-O look. Next I tried braids, but I ended up looking like Pippi Longstocking. Then I tried a ponytail, but it looked like a cheerleader's pom-pom. Putting barrettes in it just seemed to attract more attention to it. Finally I decided to just let it be Jell-O.

When Mom came home and saw me, she stopped dead. After a moment she sighed. "All right, all right, you're just expressing your independence or whatever. I'm not in a position to say anything, since I went through a stage of sporting long green fingernails."

I wanted to hug her, I was so happy at her reaction. She knew I wasn't trying to deny who I was inside. I was just trying to fit in for once.

That left one more person to face, and it was the hardest one: Nainai, my Chinese grandmother. She's always telling me how much I look like Dad, her favorite son. How would she feel, now that I had orange Jell-O hair?

I would soon find out, because Dad and I were going to the airport to pick her up this evening.

As Dad and I drove to the airport, I tried to imagine how Nainai would feel when she saw my hair. Would she think I dyed my hair so I wouldn't look like Dad anymore? So I wouldn't even look Chinese anymore?

Anxiously scanning the passengers filing out of the airplane, I finally caught sight of her slight figure. I braced myself as she approached. What would she say?

She came up to us, and walked right past me. She didn't recognize me!

"Ma!" Dad called out. His voice was higher than usual, but at least it didn't become childish.

Nainai turned around and saw him. She beamed as he put his arms around her.

"And here is Fiona," said Dad.

I gulped. "Hello, Nainai," I managed to say, and waited for her reaction.

Nainai's eyes widened as she looked at my hair. After a pause that seemed to last forever, she turned to Dad and said, "Well, at least she didn't change her features."

This was exactly what Dad had said, too. He and Nainai exchanged a glance. What did they mean?

We went to collect Nainai's baggage. Just as I expected, she had two huge pieces of checked luggage, a big suitcase and a paper carton containing Chinese groceries. For the past year, we've tried to tell her that we can buy perfectly good Chinese stuff right here in Seattle, but she still thinks we're far from civilization and need supplies of "real food" from San Francisco's Chinatown.

Dad grunted as he heaved the suitcase onto a luggage cart. I grabbed at the paper carton, and was nearly dragged aboard the moving luggage conveyor belt. Dad and Nainai hauled me back just in time.

Panting, Dad said something to Nainai in Chinese, and I knew it meant, "Mother, you shouldn't have brought all these things."

Nainai just smiled her sweet smile. She probably thought Dad was being polite, and I guessed that she would bring as much stuff next time, if not more.

As soon as we got home, Dad went into the kitchen to prepare dinner. Nainai went with him, and I could hear them talking in Chinese. Again, his voice sounded a little higher than usual. I peeked into the kitchen and found him standing by the counter, meekly listening to Nainai as she told him how to prepare one of the dishes. It would be really embarrassing if he went into his little boy act at the dinner table, when Grandpa and Grandma MacMurray were there. To my relief, Dad spoke in his grown-up voice at dinner.

When Grandpa and Grandma MacMurray visit us, Dad usually cooks dishes that are familiar to most Westerners, things like beef and broccoli or sweet-and-sour pork. But tonight the dishes he cooked used many of the new ingredients Nainai had brought with her.

"What's this?" asked Grandpa.

The thing he held up was limp, transparent, and slippery. It didn't have any flavor of its own, and you could taste only the gravy. I had eaten it before, and if I hadn't known what it was, I would have enjoyed it a lot more. I hoped very hard that Dad wouldn't tell Grandpa the truth.

But of course Dad didn't hesitate. "It's jellyfish."

"I brought it over today from San Francisco," Nainai said with a pleased smile. "You soak it until it's soft, and then braise it in soy sauce, wine, and ginger. Good, isn't it?"

Grandpa gulped and put his hand over his mouth. But he was game, and took another bite. This time he even managed to swallow.

Grandma couldn't quite control her shudder when Grandpa passed the dish of jellyfish to her. "I'll have trouble picking it up with my fork," she said, and passed it on. It was a weak excuse, and we all knew it.

Nainai looked down at her plate and didn't say anything. I felt I had to do something. I helped myself to a huge serving of the jellyfish.

"I bet some of the things we eat must seem really gross to people in other countries," I said. "Hey, we should have a contest! Let's go around the table, and each person has to think of the grossest thing that gets eaten by people."

There was a silence as we all thought furiously. Ron raised his hand first. "The French eat snails, slathered with butter and garlic."

"Not bad, Ron," said Dad. "Snails are gross enough, but snails with butter and garlic get even more points."

Mom was next. "Let's see . . . Australian aborigines eat larvae. It's an important source of protein out in the bush." She had gone to a conference in Sydney, Australia, last year.

"What's larvae?" I asked.

"They're worms," said Ron, grinning.

I remembered that when I had baby shrimp in a salad for the first time, they looked a lot like worms, and I refused to eat them. Dad didn't try to force me, but another time he served prawns, which were just bigger shrimp. I was okay with them, and after that he served smaller and smaller prawns until I got used to the idea of eating the tiny, wormlike baby shrimp. But I had to admit that real worms were a different story.

Ron seemed to be enjoying my discomfort. "Insects go through a larva stage before they go into cocoons and become fully adult." He turned to Mom. "Your larvae beat my snails."

"We eat fried grasshoppers in China," said Dad. "Those are adult insects. They're nice and crunchy, and they taste good with a dash of soy sauce."

We couldn't decide whether larvae got more points than adult insects, like grasshoppers. In the end we voted for larvae as being more gross.

"Back in Scotland, I always began my day with blood sausages," contributed Grandpa.

"Yech!" I cried. "What are blood sausages?"

"They're sausages made with pig's blood," said Grandma. "Very nourishing they are, too, especially for children who are sickly."

"I don't think you deserve lots of points, Mother," Mom

told Grandma. "Blood sausages sound bad, but they don't actually look bloody."

It was my turn, and I thought hard. I finally came up with something my friend Amanda had told me. "In Japan they eat something called *natto.* That's rotted soybeans. They're kind of slimy, with strings that are like snot from your nose. If you put some natto in your mouth, the sticky strings flop all over your chin."

I looked around at the disgust on everybody's face and thought I had won the contest for sure.

But Grandpa wasn't giving up. "Nothing can beat haggis!"

I knew about haggis, and I had to admit that Grandpa had a winner there.

"Oh, come on," said Mom. "When did we last have haggis—really?"

"I made it for Robert Burns Day only last year," Grandma said proudly.

"What is haggis?" asked Nainai.

"You take a sheep's stomach and fill it with a mixture of sheep innards, oatmeal, suet, and spices," said Grandma.

"Then you cook it for a few hours until everything is soft and mushy. You eat it with a wee dram of whisky, and there's nothing like it!"

"There's nothing like it, even without the wee dram of whisky," muttered Mom. I got the feeling that she wasn't quite as crazy about haggis as Grandpa and Grandma.

"Looks like haggis is the winner," said Dad.

But Ron wasn't giving up. "Hey, how about lutefisk?"

Lutefisk is a Norwegian dish, and it's made with salted cod. There are lots of Norwegians in Seattle, so we locals know all about it. Dad had to explain what it was to Grandpa, Grandma, and Nainai, who were from out of town. "You soak salted cod in lye for a long time, until it's nice and soft. So it has a strong taste of baking soda."

Mom grinned and added, "In texture, lutefisk is very much like a garden slug."

We decided to give the most points to lutefisk, although haggis came close. Nainai didn't look uncomfortable anymore, and Grandma made another try at eating the jellyfish.

After swallowing, Grandma took a moment to recover

before turning to Nainai. "I hope you're going to the Folk Fest with us this weekend?"

Nainai nodded. "I'm going to the children's literature session. You've heard that my son will be talking?"

"Indeed, yes!" said Grandpa.

"Fiona's father and I are going to give her a very nice surprise," said Nainai. Her eyes were bright as she looked at me.

Knowing about Nainai's "nice" surprises in the past, I wondered a little nervously what it would turn out to be this time.

Once, Nainai brought me a pair of Chinese cloth shoes as a nice surprise. They were made of silk, and the embroidery was so beautiful that it was a shame to walk in them. It turned out that I couldn't walk in them anyway, because the shoes were an inch shorter than my feet.

Nainai had shaken her head and said a few quiet words to Dad. I learned afterward that she thought my feet were enormous. Having small feet was a sign of class, and in the old days, women in China had their feet tightly bound with bandages to prevent them from growing normally. I did inherit *some* things from my mom, including bigger bones than most Chinese.

"Fiona is going to be a busy girl at the festival," said Grandma MacMurray. "She'll be in our junior troupe for the Scottish dance performances, too."

Nainai didn't know what Scottish dancing was like. "Does it involve bagpipes?" she asked. "They're very loud, and my ears hurt when I listen to them."

I admit that the pipes were something you had to get used to. But they do grow on you.

"The music isn't always from bagpipes," Mom said. "For Scottish dancing, you can have flutes, drums, fiddles, and all sorts of other instruments, too. Our troupe will just have my father's fiddle to provide the music."

"I hope you didn't mind having all those dancers here for the rehearsal last night," Grandma said to Dad. "Did the noise bother you while you were working?"

Dad smiled. "I started writing when Ron was two and Fiona only one. They made a lot more noise than all your dancers. When Fiona was hungry for her bottle, she was a match for any bagpipe."

"Too bad Ron isn't taking part in the festival," muttered Grandpa. He was still disappointed that Ron hadn't even tried on his kilt yet.

"You forget, Grandpa," said Ron. "I *am* taking part. I'll be in the kung fu competition."

Nainai smiled warmly at Ron. "I'm so glad you're interested in kung fu. Size doesn't matter there. Sometimes a small person can defeat someone much bigger."

She probably meant that as a compliment, but it was exactly the wrong thing to say to Ron. He turned a dull red and looked down at his plate.

Grandpa quickly jumped in. "What do you do at your kung fu exhibition, Ron?"

Ron looked up. "We start with an exhibition of punches, kicks, flips, and cartwheels. Then we pair off two at a time and have bouts."

"Are your bouts like the fights we saw in that martial arts film you took us to last year?" asked Grandpa.

"Don't I wish they were!" said Ron.

Grandpa frowned. "For my part, I'm glad they aren't. I was shocked at how violent things became!"

"Didn't you enjoy the fun, Grandpa?" I asked. I had

been sitting next to him during the movie, and now I remembered that he hadn't laughed at all.

Grandpa stared at me. "Do you mean to say that the film was supposed to be funny?"

We had gone to one of the Hong Kong action movies, which often include a lot of slapstick. "You mean you thought the movie was serious?" asked Ron, and he began to sputter.

We all broke out laughing, and Grandpa laughed the loudest of all. He had to make up for not having laughed during the movie. "I did think some of the scenes were funny," he admitted. "But I didn't want you to think that I found the Chinese men ridiculous."

Dad smiled. "Some of the Chinese men in that movie *were* ridiculous."

Grandpa's face became serious. "I hope you don't use those terrible weapons we saw in the film, Ron, like the two sticks connected with a chain. Somebody can get killed with one of those. In fact somebody *was* killed in the film."

"We don't use weapons at all in our bouts," Ron said. "We go empty-handed."

"There was plenty of swordplay during the Highland Games we went to," I reminded Grandpa. "Those bouts looked lethal!"

"When are your bouts?" Nainai asked Ron.

"Our school is performing from ten to twelve on Saturday morning," said Ron. "I come on around eleven."

"That's good," said Nainai. "There's no conflict. Your father's literature session is at four o'clock on Sunday."

I heard a gasp from Grandpa. "The Scottish dancing exhibition is also scheduled for four o'clock on Sunday afternoon!" he said.

There was complete silence around the dinner table. Dad finally cleared his throat. "I know how much Fiona wants to take part in the dancing. She doesn't have to go to my talk. She's heard me lots of times."

Nainai looked heartbroken. "But your surprise . . ."

"Never mind," said Dad. "There will be other occasions."

"No!" said Nainai, and I realized that she might look like a frail old woman, but she was a very determined one. "This is a very special occasion."

She turned to me. "Fiona, your father's new book

features a brave young girl who helps the dragon overcome his enemies. Your father had you in mind as a model for the girl. At his talk, he was going to have you go up on the stage to take a bow."

I was overwhelmed. Until right then, I had never really known how my parents thought about me. I knew when they were happy—when I got good grades in school and Dad gave me his slow smile, or Mom gave me a warm hug. I knew when they were mad at me—when Dad went very quiet and wouldn't look at me, or when Mom's eyes narrowed and her lips tightened. But I had never wondered what kind of *person* they thought I was. Did Dad really think I was like the brave heroine of his book?

Nainai continued, "You're supposed to wear a costume that's the same as the one your father drew for the book, Fiona. I even made the outfit and brought it with me."

"You can't let your pa down, Fiona," Grandma said to me. "We'll try to find another dancer somewhere."

I could see she was very disappointed, although she tried to smile.

Grandpa turned to Ron with a question in his eyes. But Ron looked away and wouldn't meet his gaze. Grandpa sighed. "If Fiona doesn't dance, we'll just have to find another dancer somehow and start from scratch."

There didn't seem to be any way out of this mess. Whatever I chose to do, someone was going to be unhappy.

Friday morning I rushed off to school before Grandpa, Grandma, and Nainai could get a chance to talk to me. I still hadn't decided what I should do.

I told Amanda about my problem as we were walking to the school bus. "Gee, it'd be too bad if you didn't join the dancers," she said. "You would have dyed your hair for nothing!"

I didn't need this reminder that I still had to face the

other kids in school when I arrived with my orange Jell-O hair. I was wearing a hat on the bus that morning, but that would have to come off when we entered the school.

Sure enough, there were giggles when I took my hat off by my locker. And a girl who sits behind me in homeroom asked, "What happens if you get hot? Is your hair going to melt?" But it actually wasn't quite as bad as my first day in school, when that nasty Fee-Fi Boy and his friends made fun of my name. Actually, it turned out that I wasn't the only one with dyed hair. At our lunch table, one of the other girls had bleached her curly black hair to a light brown, and there was also Harry Kim with his pale blond hair.

As I looked at Harry, I noticed that the dark roots were just beginning to show near his scalp. Pretty soon I'd have the same trouble with my own roots. In fact I was having trouble with my roots in more ways than one.

Still, I was glad when we got off the subject of hair and started discussing the Folk Fest. "You know, I like the juggling and the comedy acts outside on the lawns," said Harry. "Some of those are more fun than the organized programs indoors."

"I never miss the Celtic storytellers," said Amanda. "There's one woman who accompanies herself on a harp. I hope she's coming again this year."

"'Celtic' means Irish, doesn't it?" said another kid. "Why should you be interested in something Irish?"

"Why can't a Japanese American enjoy Celtic story-telling?" demanded Amanda.

"Scots are Celts, too," I said, "and Amanda is coming to watch the Scottish dance program."

"Say, is it true that you'll be one of the dancers, Fiona?" asked Harry.

I didn't want to tell my friends that I might not appear in the program after all. So I just said, "My grandfather is directing the junior group of Scottish dancers." I added proudly, "He used to be a really good dancer when he was young."

"Your *grandfather* was a dancer?" said one of the other boys. "I thought all the dancers were girls. I saw a picture of the Highland Games once, and the dancers all wore little skirts."

"Look, let's get this straight once and for all," I said. "The little skirt is called a kilt, and it's intended for *men*. In

Scotland, only *men* wear the kilt, never *women.*" Honestly, I was beginning to sound just like Grandpa.

"Okay, okay!" said the boy. "You don't have to get mad."

Just then, Ron walked past our table on his way to the playground. "Hey, Ron, since you're part Scotch, I bet you have your very own kilt!" said Joel, one of the other boys at our table. He was in Ron's class, and was new that year.

Joel had guessed right. Ron *did* own a kilt. But it was not something he wanted people to know about.

The boy next to Joel poked him. "Chill out, Joel. Better not mess with Ron Cheng."

Joel ignored the advice. "I bet you'd look great in one of those cute little skirts, Ron."

Ron stopped and looked at Joel. His face turned very white, and then red. "I never knew you were so fascinated by skirts, Joel," he said. "There's a sale on skirts at the mall this weekend."

Everybody at our table tensed. Whatever was going to happen, it was too late for us to stop it. With a low growl, Joel launched himself at Ron.

We were having pizza for lunch, and I had seen Ron

measuring the distance to our table, so I knew what he was going to do.

I quickly picked up my slice of pizza, just as Ron used the momentum of Joel's rush to flip him over our table. Joel lay stunned for a moment, and then struggled up. It was a mess, with spilled drinks, half-eaten apples, and paper plates all over the place. When Joel climbed off the table and made it to his feet, we saw slices of pizza stuck to his back.

"Applying for a job at Domino's Pizza?" Ron asked Joel.

The teacher who had lunchroom duty hurried over to find out what the uproar was about. By the time he heard everybody's story, the bell rang and we had to go back to our classes.

TGIF, and the end of the school day couldn't come a minute too soon for me. But my problems were not over. I still had to face my family and decide what I was going to do during the Folk Fest.

I got home at almost the same time as Ron. Grandpa and Grandma MacMurray were in the living room. "Hello, darlings," Grandma said. "You must be starved. Your pa left some raisin scones for your tea."

Dad makes great scones, better than any store-bought ones. The only problem is that he and most Americans pronounce "scone" to rhyme with "stone." When Ron and I did that, Grandpa MacMurray immediately corrected us. "To a good Scot, 'scone' rhymes with 'gone,'" he said. "Don't let me hear you say it any other way!"

But when I pronounced it that way to my friends, they laughed at me. So I try to say it the Scottish way with Grandpa and Grandma and the American way with my friends.

"Did you and Grandpa have your scones?" I asked, doing my best to make "scone" rhyme with "gone."

Grandma smiled. Maybe she noticed the careful way I pronounced the word. "Yes, darling. They were very good, too."

As I went into the kitchen, I thought about Grandma's smile. There was something sad about it. I also noticed that Grandpa didn't give us his hearty, booming laugh when Ron and I came back.

I found Nainai in the kitchen. For once she wasn't cooking. She was sitting at the kitchen table, sewing a loop for the button on a silk jacket. I caught my breath. It was the most gorgeous jacket I had ever seen, made of pale green silk, with brilliantly colored embroidery.

"Is that . . ." I had to swallow before I could continue. "Is that part of the costume you made for me to appear on Dad's talk?"

"It's the top," answered Nainai. "I made a pair of silk trousers to go with it, but they're much more plain."

Ron sat down at the kitchen table and took a big bite of his scone. "Dad told me that in the old days, Chinese women wore trousers, while the men wore those long gowns with the slits and buttons up the sides," he said. I knew he was trying to lighten things up.

Nainai nodded. "I remember my own father sometimes wore a *qipao*—that means 'Manchu gown,' you know, because they were first introduced by the Manchus in the seventeenth century, when they conquered China."

I had seen pictures of the qipao, and I couldn't believe my ears. "You mean those slinky things worn by girls trying to look sexy?"

"The ones worn by men were loose, not slinky!" laughed Ron. "I wonder how all those old kung fu masters managed not to trip over their gowns when they fought."

"So you wouldn't mind wearing a qipao?" I challenged Ron.

"It's not what you wear, but what you do that matters," declared Ron.

Nainai finished sewing on the button and folded the shiny jacket. Then she picked it up and left the room without a word. Ron and I looked at each other, then went back to munching on our scones.

I tried to do my homework on the dining room table, but I couldn't concentrate. Should I stick with the Scottish dance troupe and make Nainai unhappy, or appear on Dad's program and leave Grandpa and Grandma MacMurray in the lurch?

When Dad came home, he went into the kitchen to get dinner ready. I saw Nainai go in and join him. As I sat doing my homework, I overheard their two voices in the kitchen speaking in Chinese. Again, Dad's voice was much higher than usual.

I knew very little Chinese, but I did understand Dad when he said, *"Bu yao jin,"* which means "It doesn't matter."

Then Nainai said, *"Zhen kexi,"* which means "It's really too bad!"

So Nainai was obviously very upset, and Dad was doing his best to console her. He had to be disappointed himself at the thought that I might not be going to his talk. But instead of sounding bitter, he was doing everything he could to make Nainai feel better.

I understood that this was what Mom had meant by "filial duty." To Dad, Nainai's feelings are more important than his own. After listening for a while, I was no longer embarrassed at hearing Dad speak in his boyish voice. Mom is like a child when she's playing games at being thrifty. But when Dad speaks in his childish voice, he's really an actor playing a part, like that man in the Chinese story who babbled and drooled and crawled on the floor. He was doing it to be a good Chinese son. I was proud of how my father treated his mother, and I was glad that half of me was Chinese.

How could I be cruel enough to disappoint Nainai? But it was just as cruel to disappoint Grandpa and Grandma MacMurray. They had come all the way from Vancouver looking forward to having one of their own grandchildren dance in the festival.

Across the dining table, Ron was also doing his homework. He finished before I did, and I watched him putting away his notebooks. He was neat in all his movements—maybe from all that kung fu training.

That's when I was struck with a brilliant idea: Ron could take my place in the Scottish dancing! After all, Ron was the one Grandpa really wanted for the dance troupe, and that beautiful kilt was his in the first place. Being quick and light on his feet, Ron wouldn't find the steps of the dances too hard to learn.

"Ron," I called before he reached the door, "how would you like to take my place and join the Scottish dance troupe?"

"What?" he squawked. Actually, "squawked" isn't the right word. He squeaked. Ron's voice had changed, and most of the time it sounded deep. But once in a while, his voice still broke into a high squeak. "You're not . . ."—he stopped, took a breath, and got his voice back down again—"serious."

"It'll be perfect!" I said. "You can take my place at the

rehearsal tonight and start learning the steps. We'll be having our final rehearsal tomorrow night, so you'll get enough practice to master the dances in plenty of time for the performance."

"I've never taken dancing lessons in my life," Ron said between his teeth, "and I don't intend to start now!"

"Look, Ron," I said, "you'll be able to wear your kilt at last."

"That kilt!" said Ron. "You saw what happened at school today!"

"When we were talking about the Manchu qipao just now," I reminded him, "you said yourself that what you wear doesn't matter. It is what you do that matters."

"I don't want to spend the rest of the school year flipping people around the lunchroom," said Ron.

"Look, nobody's going to bother you after what happened to Joel, and it will make Grandpa so happy to see you wearing the kilt," I coaxed. "Plus, I'll be able to wear Nainai's costume and be in Dad's show."

"Don't you think about anything except what to wear?" demanded Ron. "First it's the kilt, and now it's that silk costume!"

I realized too late that we hadn't kept our voices down. I peeped into the living room and saw Grandpa and Grandma sitting stiffly upright on the sofa, their eyes looking straight ahead. It was clear that they had overheard.

"Listen, Ron," I said more quietly, "Grandpa and Grandma are disappointed and unhappy. Nainai is heartbroken because I might not wear her costume. We've got to do something!"

"Fiona, you must be totally insane if you think I'm going to put on that little skirt—I mean that *wee* skirt—and hop around in front of people!" snarled Ron, and he ran out before I could say anything more.

Remembering the boys in our school lunchroom, I couldn't exactly blame Ron. Hopping around in a little skirt would sound really sissy to most American kids.

Supper that night was quiet. It felt weird to have Grandpa there and not hear his booming laugh. With Nainai's help, Dad had cooked a meal that didn't include anything too strange. Maybe Nainai thought she had already made her point with the jellyfish.

We ate our way steadily through dinner, but we didn't say much. Finally Grandpa cleared his throat. "The dancers are coming over at seven-thirty tonight for another rehearsal."

Dad opened his mouth but decided not to say anything. I saw Grandpa glance at me, but I didn't meet his eyes. Nainai was sitting right across from me. If I said I would continue as one of the dancers, it would be the same as telling her that I wouldn't be wearing her silk outfit.

The meal lasted forever, and even the dessert seemed to take a long time to eat. Usually it takes me one nanosecond to wolf it down. At last we finished.

While Ron and I cleared the table and started the dishes, Grandpa and Grandma went out to the back patio and sat on a wooden bench. The bench was right outside the open kitchen window, and I could hear their voices quite clearly.

"What do you think Fiona will do?" asked Grandma. "I feel sorry for the poor lass, having to make a difficult choice like this."

I put the last dinner plate gently in the dishwasher and tried not to make any noise as I scoured the frying pan.

"We'd better let her go to her pa's talk," Grandpa said

gruffly. "We'll try to find another dancer. Someone in the senior group might know a likely youngster hereabouts."

"We can't let Fiona's pretty costume go to waste," said Grandma. "Such a lot of work her other grandma put into it."

"That kilt I brought is going to waste!" said Grandpa. Next to me, Ron froze as he was emptying coffee grounds into the garbage can.

"Our laddie hasn't shown the least interest in wearing a kilt," continued Grandpa. "He cares only about kung fu and all those Asian martial arts. He wants nothing to do with his Scottish ancestors!"

"That's not true, Alec," protested Grandma. "He loved the Highland Games! And remember the times when you held him on your lap and told stories about heroes like William Wallace and Robert the Bruce? He never could get enough of those tales, and he kept coming back for more."

"And when was the last time I held the boy on my lap?" demanded Grandpa.

I saw Ron squirm with embarrassment. He didn't want a reminder of the days when he had been a little kid sitting on someone's lap. But I suspect that he was uncomfortable for another reason. Grandpa MacMurray was right. It had been a while since Ron had shown any interest in Scottish history and culture. For that matter, I was pretty ignorant of Scottish things myself.

Mom doesn't talk much about culture or history. In fact I don't remember hearing her show any interest in history—any kind of history. Instead, she tries to encourage our interest in science and mathematics. If I ask her who the Jacobites were, she'll tell me to go look them up in the encyclopedia. But if I ask her about imaginary numbers or black holes, she'll tell me about them in detail, a lot more detail than I need.

Dad is different. He's always ready to fill us in about Chinese history or culture. Since he is a great storyteller, he makes it sound fascinating. That's why both Ron and I wound up knowing a lot more about China than about Scotland.

I've gotten into the habit of saying that I'm half and half, meaning half white, half Asian. But in appearance I was 30%/70%, and Ron 75%/25%. Culturally we aren't half and half, either. We both know much more about our Chinese half than our Scottish half. Grandpa and Grandma weren't hurt just because Ron refused to try on the kilt. They must have been really bothered about our ignorance of Scottish culture.

"The dancers will be coming any minute now, Alec," I heard Grandma MacMurray say. "We'd better go in and make ready the living room. But what are we to do about the missing dancer?"

The back door opened and Grandpa and Grandma came into the kitchen. Then Ron did something that left me speechless. He walked up to Grandpa and said, "Do you think it's too late for me to join the Scottish dancers?"

With Grandpa's help, Ron put on his new kilt. It fit him perfectly, as we all knew it would, since he was the same height as I was. Ron made a face when Grandpa hung the purse, or sporran, from his belt, but he didn't mind the Balmoral cap so much. It looked just right on his red hair—his naturally red hair.

When Ron had the whole outfit on, Grandpa stepped back and beamed at him. "There's my . . ."

Grandpa had started to say "wee laddie." I even saw him round his lips for the word "wee," but he stopped himself just in time and ended with "laddie."

Grandpa decided Ron needed some encouragement. "You know, of course, that dancing is always one of the athletic events of the Highland Games?"

When we went to the Highland Games in Vancouver, Ron didn't see any of the dancing. He spent the whole time watching the hammer throwing and the caber tossing. I saw some of the caber tossing and found it pretty weird. The caber is a great big log about the size of a telephone pole. You're supposed to raise it upright, then spin it around and try to make it fall pointing the other way. It looked totally impossible to me. In fact few of the contestants managed to do it.

After we came home, Ron found a long two-by-four in Dad's toolshed, and he tried to toss it like a caber when he thought no one was looking. But he had to give it up. I suspected that he planned to try it again when he was five years older and two feet taller—if he ever got to be two feet taller.

"You might think dancing is much easier compared to

hammer throwing and caber tossing," continued Grandpa. "But it's just as hard. Some people believe Highland dancing was really a victor's celebration after winning a battle!" Then Grandpa gave his clinching argument. "In the old days, only menfolk did the dancing. It was considered too strenuous for the womenfolk!"

That made Ron draw himself up straighter. After Grandpa's little talk, Ron was ready to accept the kilt, the cap, and the purse. But he still made a face as he tucked in the frilly blouse.

Grandpa noticed Ron's expression. "Don't sneer at the fancy lace decoration on your blouse. Bonnie Prince Charlie wore a lacy blouse with his kilt at the Battle of Culloden!"

Personally, I found it hard to believe that Bonnie Prince Charlie did any such thing. But it was true that our children's book of Scottish history had an illustration showing the prince at the battle, looking very handsome in his kilt and his lacy blouse.

"Maybe that's why he lost the battle of Culloden," said Grandma, and winked at me.

Grandpa turned bright red and drew a deep breath to

give a crushing reply, but the doorbell rang and the dancers began to arrive.

Maggie blinked at the sight of my orange Jell-O hair, but she was too polite to say anything. Then she saw Ron dressed in his Highland outfit. "Hey, is that boy going to join our troupe?"

I nodded. "He's my brother, and he'll be taking my place in the dance."

Maggie looked surprised. "Your brother? But he's got red hair!"

What she meant was that Ron had *genuine* red hair. "He looks cool in that kilt," she added.

Ron belonged and I didn't. I turned away, trying not to mind.

The eight dancers took their places, now consisting of four boys standing opposite four girls. Grandpa raised his bow. His eyes were bright as he looked at Ron in the row of four boys. He brought his bow down on the opening bars of the first reel, and soon the room began to shake again with the thumps of pounding feet.

I watched Ron gradually getting the hang of the dances. He really was quick and light on his feet, and his reflexes were good. Before long, he was swept into the dances, and he was keeping up pretty well. It seemed that Grandpa's worries were over.

As I watched the brilliantly dressed dancers whirling and spinning in front of me, I tried hard to feel glad for Ron. After all, it had been *my* idea for him to take my place.

Now I was free to put on Nainai's costume and take part in Dad's program. I left the living room, slowly climbed the stairs, and went to my room.

Nainai was upstairs sitting at my desk, reading one of Dad's Chinese paperback books. For years I thought those were serious books about philosophy or history. Then Dad confessed that they were adventure stories about outlaws and bandits, full of sword fights and chases and kung fu. When I told Ron about it, he said it was worth learning Chinese to read those books. I bet anything he'd do it, someday.

When Nainai saw me come in, she smiled and put the book down. "Ready to try on your costume, Fiona?" she asked.

She opened her suitcase and carefully took out the

shiny silk jacket and trousers. Seeing the jacket unfolded, I caught my breath again. Against the green silk material, the embroidered flowers stood out and sparkled like a garden in spring.

I took off my T-shirt and put on the jacket. Nainai laughed when she saw me inserting a button into the wrong loop. She undid the button and put it into the right loop. Then she helped me with the other four buttons.

The silk jacket felt like cool water against my skin, and it made a wonderful *swish* sound as I moved. I felt like a Chinese princess.

Then I remembered my hair and moaned. "How can I appear onstage as a Chinese girl with my orange hair?"

Nainai smiled. "No need to worry. You see, I know you have short hair, and Chinese girls in the old days wore a long braid down their back. So I came prepared."

From her other suitcase, Nainai took out a black wig with a long braid. So that was what she and Dad had meant when they said that it was all right as long as my features hadn't been changed. The color of my hair wasn't a problem for them.

After Nainai carefully fitted the wig over my head, I

turned and looked in the mirror. An elegant stranger looked back at me.

From behind me, Nainai said softly, "It's the cover illustration come to life."

I laughed. "Not with jeans!" I took off my jeans and pulled on the silk trousers. They were a little snug around the waist, but I could stand it. The trouble was that the pants were way too short.

Nainai gasped as she looked at my bare ankles showing under the pants. "Your father gave me your measurements only two months ago!"

Grandma MacMurray said I had grown three inches since she last saw me. That was an exaggeration. But I had certainly grown at least two inches since Nainai's last visit. Dad may have even given her my new measurements (at least they were new a couple of months ago), but I suspect she refused to believe them.

"Maybe I can put a border around the bottom cuff, something really pretty," said Nainai. She started rummaging around in her suitcase and took out a bag of silk remnants.

I took off the silk pants and put on my jeans again. "I

want to show Dad his book cover coming to life," I told Nainai, and went across the hall to Dad's studio.

He looked up from his worktable and grinned. "Like the costume?"

"It's gorgeous!" I told him. "But the pants are too short, and Nainai is adding some strips at the bottom to make the legs longer."

Dad laughed. "She refuses to believe that a girl can grow as fast as you do!"

"Can I look at the cover of the new book?" I asked. He doesn't show anybody his work until it's finished, but this time things were different. Since *I* was on the cover, I had a right to know what I looked like.

"All right." He got up and opened the big cupboard where he stores his folders. It's Dad's treasure chest. I've always wanted to poke around in that cupboard and look at all his pictures, both old and new. But it's strictly off-limits. Even Mom doesn't look inside without Dad standing close by.

So I eagerly peered inside while I had the chance, but all I saw were big folders, neatly arranged in the vertically divided shelves. Dad took out a folder and closed the cupboard. He untied the string of the folder and laid out the paintings for his latest book.

"I'm not finished yet," he said. "My editor says I have too many pictures crowded around the beginning of the story and not enough at the end. So I have to paint two more for the second half of the book."

He took out the picture that was to be on the cover. I looked at the girl standing next to the familiar figure of the dragon that appears in all Dad's books. Dad paints in watercolors, so his pictures are not as bright as the covers of some other children's books. But the softer colors are perfect for the clouds and mist that always swirl around his dragon. The backgrounds of his pictures remind me of Chinese landscape paintings I've seen in museums.

I stared at the figure of the girl on the cover. Was I really as pretty as that? I felt a warm glow as I realized that this was how my father saw me.

The girl on the cover was wearing Nainai's costume. On me, the unfamiliar outfit felt a little awkward, but in the picture, this girl looked graceful and comfortable. Her head was slightly bent as she looked thoughtfully at the dragon. She showed no fear, in spite of the dragon's fierce, bulging eyes, his sharp fangs, and his murderous-looking claws. Obviously, she had already guessed that he was a coward.

Next to the fearsome dragon, the figure of the girl looked dainty. Then I realized that something was not quite right: the girl in the picture had tiny hands and feet. Not only do I have fingers that are already an inch longer than Nainai's, but the size of my feet horrifies her. And of course we had just discovered that my legs were too long.

But Dad still saw me as a dainty, graceful Chinese beauty. So I hugged him. "Thank you, Dad. That's the greatest compliment I ever got in my life!"

If the Chinese prefer dainty maidens, then how did Dad happen to fall in love with Mom? Was it because she was a gifted mathematician? I didn't think it could have been Mom's Scottish accent, her long legs, her red hair, or her hazel eyes.

Then I saw the row of Dad's books on the shelf. He writes books for young people because he loves children. I remembered Mom's mischievous smile when she pulled another one of her thrifty tricks. She never gets tired of playing games, and maybe Dad was attracted to her because he saw that, in some ways, Mom would always stay a child.

Nainai came in with the pants she had lengthened. Dad only laughed when she told him what she had had to do. "Fiona can't remain a little girl forever, Ma," he said. "Let's enjoy her while we can."

So I put on the whole costume and did my best to look like a dainty Chinese beauty. Nainai wanted to teach me how to walk with tiny, mincing steps. She also told me to keep my eyes down, instead of boldly staring at the audience.

"Don't make her too timid, Mother," said Dad. "Remember, in the story she's the brave one who shows the dragon the meaning of courage."

"She still has to be modest, like a proper Chinese girl," insisted Nainai.

They began to argue, and soon they started speaking in Chinese again. For once Dad didn't use his high, little boy voice.

Since I couldn't understand them, I left the room and changed back into my regular clothes. Then I went downstairs to see how the rehearsal was going. The dancers were working on their last number, one of the slower reels called a Strathspey. I was glad to see that Ron was keeping up pretty well.

I sat down next to Grandma MacMurray and did my best not to feel left out. She put her arm around me and gave me a little squeeze. I think she knew how I felt.

By now the dancers were sure of themselves, and from the smiles on their faces, I could tell they knew they were doing a good job. Suddenly I noticed that Ron was not smiling happily like the rest. Of course he was new at the dancing, and he was probably still concentrating hard to avoid mistakes.

Then I remembered that I had had a great time from the very beginning. Maybe Ron was thinking about his kung fu competition and didn't want the dancing to tire him out for his bouts.

No, that couldn't be it, since Ron does all sorts of exercises, like bicycling or jogging, before a bout. I guess he just doesn't love dancing as much as I do.

I glanced at Grandpa, who was fiddling away. Occasionally he glanced at Ron and beamed happily as he watched his laddie treading the steps of the dance.

Grandpa didn't notice that Ron wasn't enjoying himself. In his eyes, this was his redheaded grandson doing a Scottish dance, at last.

In Nainai's eyes, I was a graceful, modest, little Chinese maiden—even with my orange hair. I guess our folks see what they want to see.

Ron's kung fu group was performing at eleven on Saturday, and he wanted to be there early to warm up. The rest of the family planned to wait until it was time for Ron's appearance before they went to the festival. But Amanda and I decided to go with Ron so we could take in some other shows first.

At first we just walked around, staring at the rows of stands that sold everything from scary African masks to silver bracelets from Mexico. On the lawn, a crowd gathered around a man wearing only a loincloth, lying on a bed of nails. It made me wince just to see him, but when he got up, there wasn't a mark on his back! Another crowd gathered around a little boy playing a violin. He was only about five years old, and he produced a scared, squeaky sound. Maybe that got him sympathy, because a lot of people threw money into his violin case.

On an open-air stage was a bunch of musicians from Peru. They wore pointed caps with earflaps and woolen ponchos woven in bright colors. They played all sorts of weird instruments. I was especially fascinated by something that looked like a bundle of small pipes tied together. It sounded strange but I liked it.

Of course we had to go listen to the Celtic storytelling. Amanda was disappointed when she found out the storyteller with the harp wasn't coming. Instead, a young girl sang sad songs in a high, sweet voice.

"What do you want to go see next?" I asked Amanda after we left the auditorium.

"Let's go to the taiko drum exhibit," she said. "My folks expect me to take in at least one Japanese show."

"Gotta do what our folks expect," I said, and we headed for the open-air amphitheater, where the drummers were scheduled to perform.

"It's true, about doing what people expect you to do," said Amanda after we got ourselves settled on the lawn. "For instance, your mom is saving every penny because her people are Scotch and they're supposed to be thrifty. When nobody's looking, she's probably throwing money away."

The idea of Mom throwing money away made me laugh so hard that I fell back on the grass. People around us stared. "No, that's just Mom being a thrifty mathematician!"

"Okay," said Amanda, "so she's still doing what people expect. Since mathematicians are supposed to be thrifty, she has to save every penny."

"Just because *some* Scots and *some* mathematicians are thrifty," I said, "you can't expect all of them to be the same."

"Yeah," Amanda said, "like Japanese housewives are supposed to be meek and follow three steps behind their husbands when they go out."

I stared. "Does your mom really do that?"

Amanda laughed. "Of course not! But once, when Dad started barking out orders at her, Mom bowed deeply, sucked in her breath, and said, 'Hai, hai!' Dad burst out laughing and stopped being so bossy."

I thought about Nainai expecting me to be a dainty little Chinese maiden, and Grandpa expecting Ron to be a typical redheaded Highland laddie. "What about people who are half and half?" I asked Amanda. "Do half of our folks expect us to behave one way, while the other half expect us to behave the other way?"

Amanda grinned. "I bet they expect you to behave one way half the time, and another way the other half of the time!"

The drummers appeared and we stopped talking. Even without knowing much about taiko, I could tell that these drummers were good. Rhythm is always what I find most exciting. Maybe that's why I like dancing so much.

There was a murmur from the crowd when the biggest drum was wheeled onstage. It was more than three feet across, and it rested on its side. According to our program, the big drum was the climax of the show, and it was scheduled to be the last piece in the program. "You mean we're already at the end of the show?" I asked, disappointed.

A man sitting in front of me turned around. "No, they're changing the order of the program and playing the big drum now. I heard that the drummer is from out of town and has to leave early to catch a plane."

The solo drummer walked onstage, stripped to the waist. He stood in front of the drum and began to whack at it with a pair of clubs almost as thick as rolling pins. He started with a few slow taps, then gradually built up the tempo and increased the force of his pounding. Swaying with the beat of the drum, I could feel the same drive that I felt during the Scottish dancing.

I also got a thrill from seeing the way the drummer's muscles rippled. Hey, maybe I could join a taiko group someday!

As the drummer came to the climax of his piece, his sticks whirled so furiously that all I could see was a blur. We gave him a big hand as he left the stage. The other players came back onstage to play on the smaller drums, but they were less exciting than the performer on the big drum.

Amanda poked me. "Say, isn't it almost time for Ron's kung fu exhibition?"

I jumped up. "Yikes! What time is it?"

Amanda didn't have a watch, either, so we asked a woman next to us for the time. "It's ten to eleven," she said.

We ran for the exhibition hall. When we got there, Mom was standing by the door looking for us. "What took you so long?" she asked.

We rushed inside and made it to our seats just as Ron's group came out. They bowed to the audience. Then the announcer called out the names of the contestants for the junior group. Ron and his opponent were next to the last pair, which meant Ron was in one of the top levels.

I looked at the boy who was Ron's opponent. He was so much taller and bigger that I got worried. Nainai had said that in kung fu size wasn't important. Still, it was a bit scary the way Ron's opponent loomed over him.

"I sure hope Ron gets his growth spurt soon," I muttered.

"Height isn't everything!" said Amanda. She always defends Ron. "Hideyoshi was one of the greatest generals in Japanese history, and he was a skinny little runt. And don't forget Napoleon. He wasn't much more than five feet!"

"You'd better not let Ron hear you say 'skinny little runt,'" I said. "And I don't think he likes to be compared to Napoleon, either."

On my other side, Dad gave me a poke and told me to keep quiet and not distract the contestants.

The bouts began. Each pair of combatants bowed politely to each other before they squared up to fight. I had seen kung fu before, so the moves weren't new to me. I was familiar with the punches, the high kicks, some delivered with the fighter turning his back. Of course in an exhibition fight, the blows and the kicks are not allowed to land and actually hurt anyone. This wasn't a bloodthirsty boxing match.

None of the bouts lasted very long. We all applauded at the end of each match as the referee announced the winner. At times I couldn't tell who the winner was until it was announced, since you never saw a loser lying stretched out on the ground.

My anxiety grew as the time for Ron's fight approached. When the two boys came out and bowed, I saw again the big difference in size between Ron and his opponent, who had a reach almost six inches longer.

But when the bout began, Ron didn't have trouble with his opponent's longer reach. He managed to get inside the bigger boy's guard and "land" a few good punches. I stifled a scream as the other boy aimed a kick at Ron's head. Ron dodged it with a spectacular backward flip, and that ended the bout. The crowd cheered as the announcer declared Ron the winner.

Amanda and I grinned at each other with relief. Grandpa MacMurray took out a grubby handkerchief and wiped his brow.

I hardly noticed what happened in the last bout, and only knew it was over when I heard the applause. After the kung fu exhibition, we all went to the side entrance to meet the team members as they came out.

Mom was the first to spot Ron, and she rushed over to give him a big hug. Grandma MacMurray was next to hug Ron, while Grandpa shook hands formally with him. But there was nothing formal about the big smile on Grandpa's face.

Ron looked around until he saw Dad. "Well done," Dad said quietly.

Amanda and I were the last to congratulate Ron. At least I did the congratulating. Amanda seemed to have lost her tongue, and simply stared at Ron with shining eyes.

"Shall we go to the food court and eat lunch?" asked Mom. "Then we can decide which of the afternoon programs we want to watch."

"Yeah, let's eat!" I said. I suddenly discovered that I was starving.

Ron is usually the first one to complain of starvation, but this time he shook his head. "If it's okay with you, I think I'd better go home and soak my ankle. It's a bit swollen."

Then I noticed that he was limping. "What happened?" I asked.

"It was the way I landed on it," he said. He looked embarrassed. "Actually, I didn't have to do a flip to dodge that kick. I was just showing off."

"Yes, we'd better get that ankle fixed by tomorrow afternoon," said Grandpa.

We all knew what he meant. You can't do a Scottish dance, especially a Highland reel, with a swollen ankle.

"We'll take you to the doctor right away," Mom said to Ron. "We have to make sure nothing's broken."

"That's a bad limp you have, Ron," said Grandpa. "Maybe you chipped a bone there."

"Better safe than sorry," said Grandma. Worry deepened the lines in her face.

"I'm all right!" cried Ron. "Leave me alone!"

Dad stepped in. "Your mother's driving Grandpa and Grandma MacMurray, as well as Amanda and Fiona. So her car is a bit crowded. Why don't you come with me and Nainai in my car? We can drop in at the clinic just for a second, okay?"

Ron calmed down and agreed to go along with Dad's suggestion. Mom asked me if I wanted to stay at the festival and take in other shows. Normally, I would have loved to spend an afternoon without grown-ups. But that day, I didn't feel like enjoying myself at the festival while worrying about Ron. Amanda felt the same. "I'd like to go home, too, Mrs. Cheng," she said.

So Mom dropped off Amanda at her house, and I went home with her and Grandpa and Grandma MacMurray. It was very quiet in the car. It stayed very quiet in the house after we got home. Nobody wanted to come right out and ask the question: Was Ron's bad ankle going to stop him from performing in the Scottish dances?

I helped Mom make lunch—peanut butter and jelly sandwiches for everybody. With Mom as the cook, this was the safest choice. I thought of all the ethnic food at the festival—Vietnamese noodle soup, Russian piroshki, grilled Polish sausages—but my mouth didn't water at the thought. I was too worried to feel hungry.

I was just setting the table when Dad, Nainai, and Ron came home. I could tell from the looks on their faces that the news was bad.

"Nothing is broken," Dad said quickly. "But his ankle is strained, and he has to take it easy."

"Ron sprained his ankle?" cried Mom. "Did the doctor put an elastic bandage on to support it?"

"It's *strained,* not *sprained,"* snarled Ron. "There is a difference. I don't have to be treated like some wounded soldier!"

Nobody ate much for lunch. It's hard to make a *bad* peanut butter and jelly sandwich, but Mom managed it somehow. Maybe she put in too much peanut butter and not enough jelly, because my mouth was pretty much glued together by the sandwich. I guess everybody else's mouth was glued together, too, because nobody talked.

We spent most of the meal stealing glances at Ron, who ate less than anyone else. Normally he can put away two or even three sandwiches, especially when they're made with grape jelly, his favorite. But that day he just picked at his food. Finally he threw down the rest of his sandwich. "How do you expect me to eat when you're all staring at me?"

He got up and tried to stomp upstairs to his room—except that he couldn't stomp. It hurt too much.

The afternoon passed very slowly. Finally I couldn't stand the gloom anymore and went over to Amanda's house.

Amanda's father was mowing their front lawn. "Hi, Fiona. Heard your brother had an accident and hurt his leg. How bad is it?"

"It's not too bad, Mr. Tanaka," I told him. "He only strained his ankle. Nothing's broken."

"Amanda will be glad to hear it." He winked at me. "Better go in and tell her the good news."

Inside the house I ran into Melissa. She still had black hair. "Sorry about your hair," she muttered, not meeting my eyes.

I wondered if she had changed her mind about dyeing her own hair after she had seen what happened to mine.

I found Amanda and her mother in the kitchen, and I told them about Ron's ankle being strained, not sprained.

"Make sure he doesn't put much weight on it for a few days," Mrs. Tanaka said. She's a nurse, so she knew what she was talking about.

"I'll tell him that," I said. "He's supposed to take part in some Scottish dancing tomorrow, but I'm not sure he'll be able to make it."

"Dancing!" cried Mrs. Tanaka. "What sort of dancing? If it's a slow shuffle, he might be able to do a few steps, but even that is taking a chance."

"They're Scottish dances," I told her. "Some of the Highland reels involve a lot of hopping and jumping, I'm afraid."

"Don't even *think* of letting him do it!" said Mrs. Tanaka. "He could tear a ligament! It may never be normal again!"

She made it sound really scary. "I'd better go home right away and tell Ron what your mom said," I told Amanda. "Otherwise he might have a bum ankle for the rest of his life."

"That's awful!" cried Amanda. "Wait, I'll come with you."

When we got home, the first person we saw was Dad. "Oh, hi, Mr. Cheng," said Amanda. "I came over to see how Ron is. Is his ankle better?"

Dad sighed. "No, it's about the same. We were just discussing what we should do."

The whole family was in the living room. Grandpa and Grandma were together on the sofa, while Nainai and Ron each had an armchair. Ron had his right leg on a footstool, but I could tell he wasn't happy about it. Dad and Mom had seats on two dining room chairs. Amanda and I plopped ourselves down on the floor.

"You can't join the rehearsal tonight, and that's final!" Mom told Ron.

Ron scowled. "I haven't been dancing as long as the others, and I need the extra practice!"

Amanda cleared her throat. "My mom is a nurse, and she said Ron shouldn't put any strain on his bad ankle for a few days!"

Grandpa sighed. "That means our laddie can't use the ankle tomorrow."

"I can stand it!" insisted Ron. "The pain is much better already!"

"You mustn't take a chance," said Grandma. "Do you think your grandpa and I would want you to dance under the circumstances?"

"I promised to join the dance, and I intend to keep my promise!" Ron said with clenched teeth.

"My mom said if you're not careful, the injury could be permanent, Ron," warned Amanda. "You might never be able to do kung fu again!"

"Let me take your place tonight, at least," I said to Ron, offering a compromise. "Tomorrow we'll see how your ankle is. If it's better, you can join the troupe again."

"What Fiona says makes sense, Ron," Dad said quietly.

"Good suggestion, Fiona," said Mom, and there were nods of agreement from the others.

So it was decided that I would take Ron's place that night during the rehearsal. What we'd do the next day was still up in the air.

As Amanda got ready to leave, she still looked troubled. "You know, don't you, that Ron shouldn't even *think* of trying to dance tomorrow?"

"I know," I admitted. "But at least I stopped him from joining in tonight."

I went upstairs and put on Ron's kilt. As I adjusted the belt around my waist, I wondered if this would be the last time I got to wear the outfit.

The dancers arrived right on time. This was the dress rehearsal, the last practice session before the performance.

When Maggie saw me, her eyes widened. "So *you* are dancing after all?"

"I'm just substituting for Ron," I said. "He's hurt his ankle, and it's too sore for him to dance tonight."

Before I could say more, Grandpa tuned his fiddle and

told us to get into position. Once the dancing started, I forgot all our worries. It felt wonderful to get into the swing again.

During our first break, Grandpa smiled around at us. "This was one of our best sessions yet. Let's hope we can do as well tomorrow."

"Hey, we might even be better than the senior group!" cried one of the boys.

"Right!" cried Maggie. "Let's show them!"

Grandpa started the music again, and we went into one of the slower Strathspey numbers. It was my favorite. The more sprightly reels were lots of fun, but I liked the slow, graceful dances better.

I was so carried away by the dancing that it came as a surprise when I realized we were about to finish our last number. At the end, our audience clapped as we lined up and bowed. I saw that Dad and Mom were beaming at us, along with Grandma MacMurray.

Ron was sitting in his armchair with his foot propped up. He was clapping just as hard as the others. I looked for Nainai to see how she felt. She was seated behind Ron, and she was also clapping and smiling.

Just before Maggie left, she turned and looked at me thoughtfully. "You're really good. You're much better than your brother."

I was so moved that I couldn't speak. Maggie smiled at me and gave my arm a squeeze. "You know, I kind of wish you'd be the one dancing tomorrow."

I found my voice. "I wish things were as simple as that."

After the other dancers had left, Grandpa began to put away his fiddle and Grandma went up to him. "Fiona is a better dancer than Ron, isn't she? He did all the right things, but when he danced, he was just doing his duty. When Fiona danced, she was doing something she loved."

She kept her voice low, but I could hear her clearly. Nainai had also overheard. As she and I went upstairs to my room, she turned to me and said softly, "You should be the one to perform with the troupe, not Ron."

Her voice was not quite steady, and I could tell that it cost her a great deal to say that. If I didn't appear at Dad's talk, what would happen to that beautiful jacket she had worked so hard to embroider, and those silk trousers she'd had to lengthen?

I shook my head. "No, Nainai. Ron is better for the dance troupe. He's got the right color hair, and he's the one Grandpa really wanted in the first place."

Nainai's sad face haunted me all night, and I didn't sleep very well. When I opened my eyes Sunday morning, I saw that Nainai's bed was already empty. I found my parents in the kitchen getting breakfast ready. The sight of their faces told me that they hadn't slept well, either.

Dad was even quieter than usual. Mom looked absent-minded as she took out the pancake mix for our usual Sunday morning breakfast. Even using a mix, she succeeded in messing up the recipe. She added twice as much milk as needed, and since she didn't leave much of the dry mix, the batter ended up watery.

"I'll do the sausages!" Dad said quickly, and grabbed the frying pan away from Mom.

The pancakes were as thin as paper and practically transparent. So I wrapped them around my sausages and made a package that turned out to be delicious.

Grandpa and Grandma had already eaten, since they always get up an hour before anyone else. I saw Grandma lean over to speak to Grandpa. "Did you find that boy who might be able to dance with us, Alec?"

Grandpa shook his head gloomily. "No, his mother said he refused to do it. There isn't enough time for him to practice, and he's too scared to go onstage at this late date."

"We'll just have to hope that Ron will be recovered, then," said Grandma. But she didn't look hopeful.

Finally Ron came down to breakfast in his pajamas, and we all turned to stare at him. His face was drawn, and I could tell that he had spent an awful night.

"Want some breakfast, Ron?" Mom asked.

"Okay," he said, looking unenthusiastically at the stack of paper-thin pancakes. He limped over to a chair and sat down. His limp was not any better—maybe even worse. There was no hope at all that he would be able to dance.

After breakfast, we held a family conference in the living room. I tried hard to come up with an idea to solve our problem, but I just couldn't see any way out.

Nainai spoke first. "Our decision is obvious. My son

can still give his talk without Fiona's appearance. But the dance troupe simply cannot perform with one dancer missing. Fiona must join the troupe."

"But your beautiful costume!" cried Grandma. "All that work you put into it!"

"I'll just have to fold it up and put it back in my suitcase," Nainai said. She wasn't able to keep the bitter disappointment from her voice.

While we were cleaning up, I got a chance to speak with Mom and Dad alone.

"I don't want to hurt anyone's feelings," I told them. "I don't know what to do."

"Just be true to yourself, Fiona," said Mom.

"Do what feels right to you," added Dad.

Amanda came over after lunch. "How is Ron? Is he going to be able to dance?"

"I'm afraid not," I told her. "We've decided that I should join the dance troupe, and Dad will just have to give his talk without my appearance."

"Too bad," said Amanda. "What will happen to that gorgeous Chinese costume?"

I sighed. "It'll just go back into Nainai's suitcase, I suppose."

"Can't you think of something?" asked Amanda. "You're always coming up with those brilliant ideas!"

But my mind was still empty as we all got ready to leave for the festival.

Sunday was the last day of the festival and the most crowded, so we had to go early to find parking.

We got there with almost an hour to spare. Normally I'd have no problem enjoying myself at the festival for an hour, or several hours. But this time it was different. This time I was a performer myself, and I wasn't in the mood to take in other shows.

Nobody else in our family felt much like watching

other shows, either, so we all wound up sitting glumly around a table in the food court, picking at food that we didn't need.

Dad had the notes for his talk in front of him. He had already prepared his talk, but now he was working on it again, adding things to make it longer. Since I wasn't going to appear onstage, he had to think of ways to fill in the extra time.

Mom was talking quietly with Nainai, trying to cheer her up. Grandpa and Grandma didn't have to worry about the dancing anymore, but they didn't look all that cheerful, either. Maybe they felt guilty because I was going to be on their program instead of Dad's.

I wasn't hungry and just pulled at a piece of beignet, a kind of New Orleans fried bread. "Careful with that powdered sugar," said Mom as a cloud of white powder rose. "You'll get it on your costume."

I was already wearing the full dancing outfit: Balmoral cap, knee-high stockings, kilt, sporran, and blouse. Some of the passersby stared at me, but there were so many other people in costume that I didn't feel too conspicuous.

The day was warm, and my outfit already felt a little

hot. I was going to be a lot hotter when I started dancing. I envied the drummer at the previous day's taiko performance, who had stripped to the waist. I giggled as I thought about how Grandpa's troupe would look if we all went topless.

Then—when it was almost too late—I finally got hit by a brilliant idea.

"Dad," I said, "you're the next to last speaker at the session, aren't you?"

Dad's eyes widened. "Yes, that's what it says in the printed program."

"Do you think you can change places with the person who's scheduled to go first?" I said in a rush.

"Like the taiko drummer!" cried Amanda.

I was practically jumping up and down with excitement. "Our junior dance troupe doesn't go onstage until the second half of the program. So if you speak first, I can appear for your talk and still have time to run over and join the Scottish dancers!"

"Good thinking, Fiona!" cried Grandpa. Grandma smiled and nodded agreement.

Mom and Ron were both beaming, too. I felt pretty proud of myself.

A wail came from Nainai. "But you won't be able to wear the costume! I left it at home in my suitcase!"

Mom looked at her watch. "There's still more than half an hour before the program begins. I have time to drive home and get the costume."

She would be cutting it close. We live in the central part of the city, not far from the university. Mom could make it back in time—if the traffic wasn't too bad.

"Fiona's idea is at least worth a try," said Dad.

So Mom hurried off to the car. The rest of us split up. Ron limped off with Grandpa and Grandma MacMurray to show them the way to Center House, where the Scottish dancing was being staged. Nainai, Dad, Amanda, and I headed for the Rainier Room, where the children's literature session was being held.

Dad spotted the writer who was scheduled to speak first on the program. He went over to her and began to explain the situation.

The writer had pink hair that looked like candy floss

being pulled by several greedy hands. Fortunately, she was not as wild as her hair, and she soon understood what Dad wanted her to do. "Okay, Frank, I'll be happy to let you go first. Besides, it gives me a little longer to prepare a talk."

"How can she be calmly standing there without a prepared talk, when there are more than a hundred people listening?" I whispered to Amanda. "Dad takes days to prepare his talks."

"I guess writers come in all sorts," said Amanda.

We still had fifteen minutes before the program began, and the hall was filling up. Dad took out his notes again and began to read them over. Now that I might appear onstage, he'd have to go back to his original talk, the shorter version. He took out his pencil and started crossing out the extra things he had added.

We had seven more minutes. "Maybe you should have asked your dad to trade places with the *second* speaker instead of the first," whispered Amanda.

I shook my head. "But then I might not have enough time to change back into my Scottish outfit and make it to the dance troupe."

As it got closer to the time for the speakers to go onstage, I fidgeted so much that I was practically dancing a Scottish reel all by myself. "Is Mom going to make it?"

"Maybe she's driving around and around looking for a parking meter with time left on it," said Amanda.

"No, she isn't!" I protested. "Saving money is a game with her, but she wouldn't pull one of her thrifty tricks when things are desperate."

With five minutes to go, there was still no sign of Mom or the costume. I started to lose hope.

"Too bad," sighed Dad. "I guess Mom didn't make it." Nainai's shoulders drooped.

Dad took out his notes again and began to erase the crosses on the things he had crossed out. Which of the two talks was he going to give? Whichever one he gave, he was still going on first.

Our time was up. Mom still hadn't arrived.

Dad joined the other speakers who were lining up, and they began climbing up to the stage. They sat down on a row of chairs behind a long table.

Nainai, Amanda, and I turned sadly and started to leave the changing room. We'd have to join the audience and find seats.

"*Psst,* over here!" said a voice. It was Mom!

"You made it!" I cried.

"I got a flat tire and had to flag down a taxi," explained Mom. "You wouldn't *believe* how much it cost! But it was worth it."

So I was right after all. Mom is willing to spend good money when she knows we're counting on her.

Mom held out the costume. "Better hurry up and change!"

I tore off the fancy blouse and kilt and thrust my arms into the sleeves of the silk jacket. In my hurry to put on the pants, I stuffed both feet into the same leg. Amanda helped to pull the pants off, and I started over again. Nainai did the buttons of the jacket for me.

I turned and headed for the stage, but Mom held me back. "You can't go out with that hair!"

Fortunately she had remembered to bring the black wig. Nainai helped me cover my orange Jell-O mop with the wig.

Out front, the moderator for the session stood up to introduce the first speaker. "Ladies and gentlemen, I have the great honor to introduce the distinguished author and illustrator of books for young people—Frank Cheng."

Dad walked up to the podium, arranged his notes, and began his talk. He didn't know that Mom had arrived with the costume, so he gave the second version of his talk, the one that didn't include my appearance.

"My daughter was supposed to appear onstage, dressed as the heroine of the book," he said. "But because of a conflict, she can't make it."

Mom gave me a push. "Go on!"

I took a deep breath and slowly climbed the steps up to the stage. I arrived behind Dad just as he was saying, "So you'll have to use your imagination instead and visualize the girl coming forth . . ."

The audience pointed at me and broke out into laughter and applause. Dad whirled around. When he saw me, his jaw dropped. It was one of the few times I've seen him totally speechless.

I grinned at the audience. Then I walked slowly back and forth across the stage to let people admire the costume, and to let Dad recover himself.

Dad finally snapped his jaw shut and cleared his throat to continue his talk. "You people have a pretty powerful imagination!" he said, and another ripple of laughter came from the audience.

I flashed around one last grin and began to climb back down the stairs. Nainai would probably say that a modest Chinese maiden shouldn't grin at crowds like that, but I didn't care. I was half and half, and one half of me wanted to grin.

Backstage, Mom, Nainai, and Amanda helped me take off the silk costume and put back on the kilt, blouse, and cap. The other half of me was back in business. Amanda and I quietly left through a back door and ran for the Center House.

We found that the senior dance troupe was still doing their last number. When I joined the other junior dancers, Grandpa gave me a big smile. There was so much delight on his face that it made up for all the hurt I had felt when I thought he really wanted Ron in the dance troupe.

The senior troupe left the stage and we took our places. Behind me I could hear Grandpa tuning his fiddle.

The audience was quieting down as they waited for us to begin. It was a pretty good crowd.

Standing opposite me onstage for the first number was Maggie. When she met my eyes, she smiled and gave me a thumbs-up sign. Then Grandpa raised his bow and struck up the music for the first reel. Our feet began to tap in time to the lively tune, and at Grandpa's signal, we threw ourselves into the dance.

The night before, Grandpa had said that the rehearsal was the best session he had yet with his troupe. That day we were even better. As I passed Maggie in one of our loops, she gave me another smile and again raised her right hand with the thumb up. Then I saw that the rest of the dancers were also giving each other the thumbs-up sign. I don't think Grandpa even noticed, because he was totally caught up by the music. Just as I was totally caught up by the dance—both halves of me.

All this time, I had been assigning percentages to myself and to others of mixed race based on how they looked. What a stupid waste of time!

It didn't matter whether I looked Chinese or Scottish,

or whether I had black hair, red hair, or orange Jell-O hair. Ron had genuine red hair, but he wasn't as good a dancer as I was. I might look like an Asian girl with dyed hair and a borrowed kilt, but I could really dance a Highland reel.

That evening, after the festival was officially over, there was a party for the program participants and their friends. We were urged to go in our costumes. So again I had to make my choice: Should I keep the kilt and blouse on, or should I change into Nainai's Chinese costume?

"You might as well keep your dancing costume on," Dad told me. "You've already showed off the silk outfit."

"Yeah, that was quite an act you put on for your dad's talk," said Amanda. "You looked like a fashion model parading down the runway."

"But the people at the party will expect to see the girl on the book cover," said Nainai.

Ron suddenly spoke up. "Let me wear the kilt."

For a moment we just stared at him. Ron continued, "It's not going to hurt my ankle, since I don't have to dance."

I saw Grandma blink and take out a handkerchief to wipe her eyes. Grandpa's eyes were not quite dry, either, and when he spoke his voice was husky. "That would be very nice, Ron."

So that was how we wound up: I was in Nainai's silk outfit, and Ron was Grandpa's redheaded laddie in kilt and blouse and Balmoral cap.

When we reached the hall where the party was being held, Maggie and the others in our dance troupe didn't recognize me at first. They crowded around me to examine the costume. "Hey, I like that orange hair with the green silk," said one girl. "It's cool!"

That wasn't how Nainai felt. She wanted me to put my black wig back on, but I refused. With the wig on, I felt hot, not cool.

Helping myself to food and chatting with the others, I soon gave up my dainty Chinese maiden act. It was hard to keep it up, with my feet too big and my legs too long.

I glanced over at Ron and saw that he was showing a couple of boys some kung fu hand movements. It looked kind of strange with Ron wearing his Highland outfit.

That's when I realized I was probably the only person

in the whole Folk Fest who'd gotten to participate in two programs for two different cultures. And it had happened because I don't fit into a box or a category. I wasn't 100% anything—except myself. Our grandparents expected us to belong to one category or another. I looked more Asian, so Nainai saw me as a Chinese maiden. Ron looked like Mom's side of the family, so Grandpa saw him as a red-headed Highland boy. But inside we were just ourselves. Mom and Dad knew that, and that's all they ever wanted us to be.

I might not always blend in, but for the first time it didn't bother me. I decided that I would check the 'Other' box as my race after all when I filled out the recreation center form. It wouldn't make me an outsider or a weirdo. Everyone's got something that makes them different: the way Mom is thrifty, the way Dad uses baby talk around Nainai. Since I didn't fit in one of the boxes for race, I didn't have to choose one culture over another.

I got to be both: half and half.

ABOUT THE AUTHOR

LENSEY NAMIOKA has written many popular books for children, including *Yang the Youngest and His Terrible Ear*, a 1995 nominee for the Young Reader's Choice Award; *Yang the Third and Her Impossible Family; Yang the Second and Her Secret Admirers;* and *Yang the Eldest and His Odd Jobs*. She is also the author of two young adult novels: *Ties That Bind, Ties That Break,* an ALA Top Ten Best Book for Young Adults, and its companion, *An Ocean Apart, a World Away.*

Lensey Namioka lives in Seattle with her family.